The Red Dagger Society

Society

James W. Cameron III

DEDICATION

For Margaret, Adrian, Evins and Bill who always inspire me.

ACKNOWLEDGMENTS

Cover design by   Steve Mousourakis at
bighousegraphix (thinkbhg.com)

CHAPTER ONE

I should have seen it. I would have, too, except I was clutching my jacket so tightly, my logger's hat pulled low against the blowing sleet and snow. There was a developing confrontation between two figures a few feet away on the other side of University Avenue. As it was, my eyes watered from the cold and I kept my head down. This storm coming so late in the season had been a surprise especially to the trees that were just beginning to flower. A frozen wind like this could cut to the bone. As I made my way, my thoughts wandered like ghosts on the highway to Montgomery to the many times I had walked this same path as a student only a few short years ago and those wonderful people I had encountered along the way especially the omnipresent black Labrador retrievers. I continued my pace as briskly as possible past the spruce and fir sentinels on either side of the Avenue hulking like ancient sleeping Ents. I had a premonition that something wasn't right. Something was out of balance.

Female visitors had made complaints of unsavory behavior by some of the frat boys on campus, and that led me that snowy evening to the Kappa Zeta and Sigma Delta fraternity houses situated on the edge of campus before it creeped out to rock bluffs and then began to drop off the mountain into the fertile farmland and forest below. Occupied with my own visions of times past, I completely missed the event unfolding on the other side of the street that would so dominate my life for the next several weeks, and affect so much of the University community as we knew it. We would look back on these events as a challenge to what was most dear at this school with the humor of hindsight.

It was a late winter Party Weekend at the University where I was the newly appointed Associate Dean of the College, thirty years old, freshly out of law school, two years at Keeble College at Oxford, England followed by a judicial clerkship with the Sixth Circuit Court of Appeals. Normally, I would have been practicing law in some prestigious firm in a large city with a professional baseball team, but when the Presiding Bishop called, his entreaty was an offer I could not refuse. He had raised me after the death of my parents in a car accident when I was ten years old, and I owed him a lot. While he appeared almost frail, Bishop Cravens had the toughness of a battle worn general and when necessary could emanate a power that quelled all opposition. Fiery Bishops were like that. He needed me and it was my duty to respond. I was called and presented the opportunity to participate in a major transformation of this liberal arts college. As it was put to me, "We have a concern that a new direction is needed in the administration of the college. We have prayed and providence tells us that you would be the man for the job." Coming from the Presiding Bishop, that's powerful stuff even if I didn't love him as a father. In the language of the Church I had been "called" into service. The Clerics ran one part of the governing body of the school but the Board of

Trustees were all laymen and they controlled the money.

The school sat carved in sandstone on the peak of the southwest Cumberland Plateau, isolated physically and surrounded by thousands of forested acres. Its academic reputation was as prestigious as anywhere in the country for the liberal arts. The Mountain had a profound effect on me and had changed the direction of my life. It was where I came to grow into a man and to love the written and musical word. In the rocky mountainous soil my roots had spread wide and deep clinging to an experience made more delicious by the winds of time that swept across the crest of the plateau.

My tenure at the University as a student had been exemplary with me serving as the student representative to the Board of Trustees enabling me to know several of the sitting members at the time of my appointment, but I still wondered why had I been chosen for this task? This appointment had been quite unexpected, and interrupted my legal career, but a sense of duty and commitment to the principles of the school set me on the path back to the mountain and to Tennessee. All this rumbled around in my head like gems in a polishing drum as I made my way down to the first of the fraternity houses on my list.

The complaints I was to check out, although seemingly unrelated, had been reported to the Associate Dean of the College for Women's Affairs, and by her to me. Thus, it was my responsibility to investigate and report back to her and ultimately to the President who served as CEO of the school. The Dean of the College was away on a sabbatical until the fall semester, so I was on my own fresh as a green pea in the spring. His only advice prior to leaving was "Don't fuck up." I guessed that like pornography, you generally recognized a screw up the moment it occurred.

The "boys will be boys" attitude that had prevailed on the mountain for decades was no longer the rule. Political correctness and the admission of women had forever changed this policy, and complaints of the nature reported tonight were examined quite seriously. The details of the complaints presented to me were sketchy, something to do with a purse and something about a near rape. Neither of the girls involved were students here but rather guests from an all female college up east making the entire process more delicate since in time I would also be dealing with the Dean of Students at another college, who would undoubtedly be on a crusade seeking justice for her girls.

Architecturally, our school was modelled after English universities at Oxford and Cambridge with stately cut sandstone buildings and the occasional ivy dripping from an arched portico. We were not large, only a couple of thousand students, creating a close atmosphere where most students and faculty knew each other personally or by reputation. Traditionally, the school had emphasized the liberal arts but in recent years the sciences had become more credentialed especially with the addition of a computer sciences department. Students who did well here would compete very aggressively in any profession. Technically, the U.S. Episcopal Church owned the school having placed it here after the Civil War. The intent of the Bishops had been to locate a southern school of higher education near the confluence of the major southern railroads. Staring at a map they pinpointed Chattanooga and set about acquiring the land. They were close. The railroads converged in Atlanta, increasing the physical isolation of our campus.

My path led along University Avenue, a wide street serving as the main entrance to the school along which were staged fraternity houses, dormitories, a speckling of private homes, and ultimately the cathedral and academic buildings situated around a grassy quadrangle guarded by muscled oaks. As I continued through the dressing of oaks and evergreens I could see the glow of a few lights twinkling orange from unshuttered windows. Since street lights were infrequent except in the center of campus, I passed into and out of the shadows formed by the dark snow cloaked trees. My breath came in icy puffs and occasionally I slapped my arms to confirm they had not frozen stiff. Soon I neared the Kappa Zeta house. Deep booming music reflected off the branches and the wind was starting to pick up again. The snow and sleet now covered my coat like one of the branches of the huge firs I was passing. My charge was clear, but not to be enjoyed. No one in a party mood would want to see me this night and I didn't want to be out in this weather either.

As I approached the KZ house red and blue lights of a Sheriff's patrol car parked on University Avenue near the front walk of the fraternity house presented a kaleidoscope of added sparkle to the drifting snow. I could see the officer was in his car and someone was immobile in the back seat. The passenger window rolled down as I approached and from inside Officer Yogi Baker said "Get in, Jack. We need to talk."

Yogi and I graduated from the University in the same year. He was one of the few locals who attended this college, since most either chose not to go to college or matriculated to the University of Tennessee in Knoxville or Chattanooga. Like me, he had attended a rural public high school in middle Tennessee where few of our high school classmates even went to college. Yogi and I found that we were not from the same social order as most students here. We were not the children or grandchildren of southern aristocracy. If our ancestors had been planters, they would surely have been share croppers. Arriving here as teenagers, we grew into tall slender saplings and shared the bond of place with each other student at the University. As Southern boys we knew that geography of home inspired and defined who we were and who we would become. Each of us was infused with an oral family history that stretched back two hundred years in the communities into which we were born, among the farmers, gamblers, drinkers and the rest. This bond of commonality should have dissolved petty social differences producing a love for what the University embraced and taught. Each of us had the same mountainous dirt beneath our fingernails and it never completely washed off. Like most of my classmates and friends who attended the University, my time here was one of the most special experiences of my life. It was not so with everyone, and this is a story of such a failure.

After graduation Yogi stayed in the area and joined the Sequoyah County Sheriff's Office becoming the Chief Detective in only two years. We had remained friends, were both single, and still went on white water canoe trips on the Cumberland Plateau and in western North Carolina. I trusted him as one would trust a brother, each of us covering the others' back. We were able to communicate more by acts and deeds than verbal expression. Each of us knew the other would be straight, strong and true.

Tall with broad but slender shoulders, Yogi's reddish hair was close cropped, military style, and he spoke with a bit of a back woods inflection. "Nice", "white" and "rice" all rhymed coming off Yogi's tongue. Yogi fit right in with the local Sheriff's department where his uncle, Buford, was Sheriff presiding over a small corps of men who would have been loggers if not for law enforcement. Despite his Appalachian accent, Yogi had a keen eye for detail. Others often misjudged Yogi and underestimated his talents. He let them run with that misconception like a smallmouth on a crank bait.

Sliding into the passenger seat of the police cruiser, noticing that Yogi had cranked up the heat, I unwrapped my tartan scarf to the aroma of stale alcohol and glanced over into the rear seat as Yogi began:

"Jack, meet Bruce Sidwell. Bruce, this is Jack Mathews, who, if you don't know is the Associate Dean of the College. Bruce are you awake?" Yogi said as he reached back and shook the comatose student. "Shit" said Yogi. When Bruce failed to respond, Yogi went on, "I hope that peckerwood doesn't puke in my squad car. I'm getting real tired of cleaning up frat boy puke."

"Yogi, what is this well-bred although drunk, young man doing in your custody?" I queried.

"Story is the he threw up in a girl's purse at the KZ house."

"Did what?"

"Bruce the Purse here, allegedly barfed in a girl's purse."

"Oh my God, is she a student?"

"Oh, no, nothing that easy. She's from Yearwood College in Virginia. Down here for party weekend with sorority sisters."

"This isn't going to be pretty."

"That's what the young lady thought when she

went to powder her nose and found the winning prize."

"How did you come to hook him up?" I asked.

"I responded to a call from dispatch. Guys inside the KZ house pushed this guy onto the porch saying "here's your man.""

"Did you talk with anyone else?"

"Not yet, when I heard you had been called I decided to wait. Seems like more of a school issue than one for the Sheriff's department to handle. You know, we haven't had a good story about crap since the Bunch-Nichols turd back fifteen years ago. Remember that? A turd in the classroom building restroom so large it wouldn't fit in the toilet? Remember, the Betas were selling tickets just to come see it?"

"Jeez, I remember. Somebody's going to be upset about this."

"You mean like the President?"

"And, the Board of Trustees, the administration of Yearwood College, all those politically correct souls who would treat this as an assault on women in general, and, naturally, the *Purple Onion* staff." The student newspaper, the *Purple Onion* relished in stories of misconduct on campus loving to poke the frat system and the school administration in the eye whenever possible. The motto "If it smells, we tell..." on the masthead burned like a torch in the breast of each of its reporters. They were passionate little buggers, and a glorious pain in the ass to the Administration.

" I guess that's why you get the big bucks, buddy."

Opening the door a clump of snow hit me square in the back of my neck as it slid off the top of Yogi's car. Now I was wet and cold. As I twisted up and out of the patrol car I brushed the snow off my neck. Time to get on with it. "Let me go in and see if anyone is sober enough to tell me what happened. I'll call you tomorrow."

"Later," Yogi said and eased away from the curb. The Sheriff's Department where Bruce the Purse would sleep off the night was about ten miles away down the mountain in an old jail where I was not sure there was glass on the windows. Welcome to rural east Tennessee, Mr. Sidwell.

CHAPTER TWO

I had always considered the KZ's to be a bit unreconstructed. Most members came from Mississippi, the Alabama black belt, and southern Georgia where, as the children of southern planters, in the old days they were sent north to avoid mosquitoes and malaria. Confederate battle flags were in full display both inside and outside this fraternity house declaring their allegiance even now. Today, I mostly preferred mosquitoes over these pricks. As I approached the porch, or perhaps the veranda, the lights and sound from inside told me a live band was in full throttle and the party was on. Knocking at the front door would have been pointless since I could feel it vibrating, so I opened the door and squeezed my way into the crowded room full of sound and motion and pulsating bodies. The partygoers paid me little attention. After all, my coat and hat created the image of a character on the old *Bob Newhart Show* television show not reflective of someone in authority. I was not much older than any of them, especially the ones who were making a career out of college. One KZ had been on campus for eight years, surpassing the 7 year record held by a previous member of this same fraternity. After bumping into too many dancing couples, I grabbed one student's arm and said "Can you direct me to any officer of this fraternity?" He shouted something and pointed to the opposite side of the room where an imposing young man stood like a patrician monument. He seemed above the chaos or in charge of it. At least six feet five, I realized I would be looking up at him our entire conversation. It's hard to maintain a posture of authority when you give up five inches.

After shaking hands I said I was Jack Mathews, Associate Dean of the College. He introduced himself as Winston Campbell and guided me into the kitchen area where we could hear only slightly better. Vibrating base chords could be felt in the walls, floor and ceiling. The kitchen lay off the party room but getting into the kitchen involved a degree of body contact, pushing and several "excuse me's". The flow of bodies continued into the kitchen where counters were piled high with beer bottles, red Solo cups, and a large punchbowl full of a red mixture. The amplitude of the band was only slightly dimmed and it was still hard to talk above the noise. The thumping of the bass was primal.

"Mr. Campbell, let me get to the point. This is not a social call. I have received a report that someone at this party puked in a girl's purse." I spoke with all the authority I could muster under these circumstances.

After a soft chuckle and with feigned surprise, Campbell said "You must be mistaken. No such thing has happened at the KZ house tonight. We are all gentlemen here. Can I offer you some punch?"

"Are you sure?" I asked and paused for dramatic effect, " We received a complaint from a young lady who is a student from Yearwood here for the weekend." I stood there looking up at Mr. Campbell taking his measure. Coolly, he looked back and spoke unfazed by the accusations.

"I am not familiar with what you are referring to and I am pretty sure there are no Yearwood girls at this party."

" I spoke with Deputy Baker out front who said several members of this fraternity pushed a Mr. Bruce Sidwell onto the porch and said "he's your man.""

Campbell replied, "Bruce had already puked once on the dance floor and once in the bathroom, we just wanted him out of the house. I'm sure he has done nothing wrong. Bruce is one of our pledges and is from a good family, an English major here. I'm sure he is guilty of nothing more than too much Artillery Punch." By now Campbell was looking down his Roman nose at me.

"Artillery Punch?" I asked, being unfamiliar with the term.

" Yes, it is a KZ tradition. We have a special recipe made up for this party. The story is if you don't want to drink it, you can use it to prime a cannon." Campbell gave a hearty laugh then slapped me on the back and I knew I was going to get nowhere tonight with this crowd. I once again refused a cup of the red mixture that seemed to swirl as if a creature was swimming below the surface in the cut glass bowl. I did a double take at the movement. Deep reverb from the bass guitar in the other room caused the punch to ripple in harmonic response to the beat but that was more of a mathematical event than the freestyle movement I had observed moments before.

"Mr. Campbell, I trust you will make yourself available tomorrow if I need to speak with a representative of your fraternity," I asked.

"Of course, Dean Mathews. You are new aren't you?"

"Well, yes."

"I remember my father telling me about you. My dad is the Chairman of the Board of Trustees, you see." He paused to be sure I had understood him correctly. We stood looking at each other for a few seconds before I took my leave. I didn't know if he was going to look down at my feet to see if I had shoes on or what.

"Well, thank you for your time, Mr. Campbell. I will find my way out."

Meanwhile the pulsing chaos inside the KZ house continued with little awareness that I had even been there. I wondered why Winston Campbell had felt it necessary that I knew his father was a big shot. I had already decided Mr. Winston Campbell., the third, or fourth or fifth and I were not likely to become friends. His kind and my kind were from different planets. Yep, I'll take the mosquitoes any day.

The Bishop had given me a set of goals which included more focus on academic life, honor above all, public service and environmental awareness. The leadership of the Church was very politically correct these days. I didn't know if I was up to it, or that the students really wanted to refocus away from the reputation of a professional drinking school, but that was my challenge. I had never failed at any project and did not plan to now. I would do my job no matter the consequences. There was a time when I would have been well into party weekend myself. Now that I was part of the administration I had a completely different perspective. From the outside looking in I couldn't find the attraction in all the drinking and way too loud music. Fat, drunk and stupid had no appeal.

When I had been a student we had taken advantage of all the outdoor activities the isolated campus offered from hiking and biking trails, to caving, camping and my specialty, white water paddling. For some reason the paddling club had lost its faculty sponsor and had begun to flounder. It was one of my projects to kick start that program and with Yogi's skill we could paddle all over the Cumberland Plateau. The school even had a room full of canoes and kayaks along with paddles, pfd's and all the gear we would need. The first break we got in the weather and we would be off. The winter moisture generated three hundred miles of paddling streams on the Plateau. There weren't many schools in the country that could match that resource.

The KZ room throbbed and undulated with music and the languid movement of bodies as I adjusted my cap and squeezed back out into the night.

CHAPTER THREE

So I had struck out at the KZ house. I guess I hadn't expected much else. No frat guy was going to rat out a frat brother, although a colossal puke in a girl's purse could achieve legendary status in the telling. If so, it would be hard for the perp to remain silent. How often does a college frat boy become the fabric of legend? If Bruce the Purse was our guy, I felt that sooner or later the truth would out, perhaps even before he left the Northwoods jail. The Legend of Bruce the Purse would spread across campus although his celebrity status may not ultimately bring him the respectability he wanted. Notoriety and respectability are quite different.

The heat from the KZ house had provided a momentary insulation from the biting cold that enveloped me as I crossed University Avenue in pursuit of the second useless leg of my investigation. I once again bundled up and recalled this as a typical party weekend on the Mountain where occasionally a guy could sober up to find himself frozen on a park bench covered with snow only then wondering where was the blind date who had abandoned him. Even with the admission of female students, party weekend attracted many girls from other campuses who for generations had migrated to our professional drinking school for the legendary parties. My next stop, the Sigma Delta house where several of the members were football players, and members of other athletic teams on campus, was across and down University Avenue. Along with the Deltas, the KZs were the two most heavily dominated "jock" fraternities.

The report had been that a visiting student, again from Yearwood, had been nearly raped or at least "hunched" on the front walk leading up to the Sigma Delta house. I approached up the long stone walk leading to a massive front door complete with a large round metal knocker. Inside, I found that things were much more sedate that my last stop. No band was playing but the jukebox blasted an old Lynyrd Skynyrd tune about two steps or something. Couples were hanging around drinking and laughing but there were clearly many fewer people here. Once inside I smelled the expanse of wood that decorated the walls, floors and ceilings of every room. While spilled beer accented the floors, the walls had all been paste waxed by pledges before the weekend started. I could taste the medievalness of it all.

I scanned the room and asked one student who was helping hold up one of the waxed walls, "Where is everybody?" He mumbled something about another meeting. This guy was so drunk I was sure I had misheard him and asked if the fraternity president was around. Just before he bent over and puked against the wall, he said "No. He's gone.. Another..." I couldn't make out the end of his sentence. There were so few people at the Sigma Delta house it was not distinguishable from a normal weekend. Yet, this was Party Weekend, one of two held each year and things should have been rocking. I rounded a corner where a set of steps led up to the second floor. A solitary young man was leaning against one of the waxed walls. As I approached he held out a hand and said, "Sorry, but the womb room is occupied."

"Excuse me," I protested. He was obviously the gate keeper.

"There's a couple up there who want some privacy," he replied.

At this point I had enough and knew nothing productive would come from the Sigma Delta house on this night. Even though I had attended this school I was not pleased with what I had seen so far on this party weekend. Maybe it was time to crack down on the drinking. Anyway, I was dead tired and before I got puked on, I headed back to the small house I rented on a side street off University Avenue. Leaving the Sigma Delta house I passed few other wanderers since most had settled in to party at a particular fraternity house and would not be leaving until the snow let up in a few hours. The sidewalk crunched under my feet and occasional snow packs the size and shape of cereal boxes fell from the fir limbs.

My cottage dated to the 1930's when many of the private homes on the Mountain were built using the local sandstone material. The structures were solid but possessed few interesting architectural features. Because the University/Church owned all the land everyone leased their houses on campus. My house had a living room, a couple of bedrooms, a modest kitchen, and a dining room that opened onto a small deck in the back. The house was situated along Alabama Avenue where the houses were all modest, well treed, and with just enough separation one house could not hear what was said in anyone else's back yard. My key opened the door and I was immediately assaulted by Rocket, my year old Golden Retriever, who with my cat, Sampson, constituted our "family". Rocket put her paws on my chest and begged and begged to go play in the snow. I let her out but remained on the front stoop wrapped in my coat and scarf, while she ran and jumped and bit at the snow, occasionally running her nose like a snow plow along the grass. This dog filled my heart. I could talk to her like a best friend and she always accepted my conversation without criticism or judgment. Whatever I said was ok with her. Finally, she remembered she was hungry, took a quick pee and came in. Sampson sat in the window and just stared at such a stupid display. He was always a harsh judge of Rocket's youthfulness.

As I fixed Rocket's dinner, I punched the "play" button on my answering machine. I had two messages. The first was from Emily Sellars, Associate Dean of the College for Women's Affairs wanting me to call her about my investigation. The second was an odd thing. A girl's voice said in hushed tone," They've got him. Oh God. They took him.." Followed by a scream. There was no caller ID or other way for me to follow up on that call. It was unsettling but could have been a drunken prank. One never knew on a party weekend when mischief was afoot. I decided to change clothes and fix a drink before returning Ms. Sellars's call. From past experience I knew the call might not be pleasant. I was attracted to Emily but she could be a pain in the ass. Perhaps a tumbler of Jack Black would facilitate that conversation.

I put more wood on the fire and after changing, I poured a silver mint julep cup of fine bourbon. How to describe Jack Black? A near perfect drink, Tennessee's finest, and how do you know exactly how much is just enough? I called but got Ms. Sellars's answering machine. I left a message I would catch up with her tomorrow. What would have prompted that second call?

Thawing out with the crackling fire and Jack Daniels I picked up the latest Joe Pickett novel by C.J. Box and escaped into the wild country of Wyoming. I had passed up an opportunity to practice in the town of Buffalo at the eastern foot of the Bighorn Mountains, but vowed to get back out there whenever possible. Joe Pickett, Jack Daniels and I spent several winter evenings together. The weather outside my door this night was not unlike what the author described in the wilds of Wyoming.

Later, when I let Rocket out for the last time, snow was still falling in the stillness of the night air. Party sounds still wove among the trees but I was glad finally to be indoors warm and with my four legged friends. Others, I would soon learn were yet in the night and up to no good.

CHAPTER FOUR

My customary office hours are 8:30 until about 3 pm. Rarely do I encounter students at my door early in the morning, and today was no different. Classes begin at 8 am and continue until around 2 pm when labs and athletic training begin. As Associate Dean I am the liason between the President, the Board of Trust and the student body yet none of these constituencies consider me their friend. Some consider me their employee. None consider me their advocate, although I am squarely in the middle of any student or faculty controversy and expected to resolve all things. When I accepted the position I should have considered the untenable political position I was in, but I was too naïve at the time to understand. That would change.

I also am able to teach one course per semester. The choice is all mine, I am told, but I wonder if they mean it. I think it is going to be fun to shake up a few things here so for the spring semester I have chosen "Criminal Studies" based upon a law school class I took. Nothing like that has even been attempted here, and from what I hear the class is full. I was planning to stage a murder for the first day of class to electrify the students in their analysis of a crime capturing their interest from the first bell.

The secretary I share with the Associate Dean, Ms. Sellars, is Tammy Algood. Mrs. Algood lives just off the Mountain and has lived in Sequoyah County all her life. Her husband, Leon, a big raw boned man, works for the university land maintenance crew and helps me look out after a few acres I inherited on the edge of the mountain near the Forestry Cabin which is owned by the school. Like several others locals I have come to know, Leon Allgood could trace his roots back to the Chickamauga Cherokee who had lived nearby at the towns of Nickajack and Running Water.

My office suite consists of a small waiting area with a threadbare sofa, two offices (one for me and one for Ms. Sellars) and a desk for Tammy with a side table. The wood floors are covered with a well worn blue and cream Persian rug. Decorating the walls are photographs of various creeks and rivers Yogi and I have paddled. On this wall a photo of me running Baby Falls on the Tellico, on that one a picture of me and Yogi catching eddies at Lesser Wesser on the Nantahala. Nothing fancy just action shots caught in slo-mo of me and Yogi having fun and acting stupid. In one shot you could see our crazy paddling buddy coming through Lesser Wesser standing up in his solo canoe and catching every eddy. What's the old line, "If you are going to be stupid, better be tough!"

As I stepped into the outer chamber, my assistant said "Ms. Sellars is waiting. She has been waiting for some time."

"Thank you, Tammy," I said in passing. Tammy and Yogi spoke like they were from the same tribe.

My door was cracked open and as I entered I saw Ms. Sellars sitting straight backed in one of my English parlor styled chairs her raven black hair falling across her shoulders. Very nice but quite formal. "Good morning, Emily."

"I trust you have some answers for the horrible things that happened last night." She shot back with no foreplay. Emily was like that. Pretty damn direct.

"Emily, as you know, I froze my butt off when I went out to each of those fraternity houses to see what I could find. I understand the KZ house incident involved a purse?" I asked.

"Yes, a most horrible obscene thing. How crude." She replied.

"And, the Sigma Delta incident was a "near" rape?"

Emily said, "The hysterical girl who called me reported that a student had jumped on her back and "hunched" her like a male dog, all the way down the sidewalk. She came apart and was horrified. Both of these girls were from Yearwood and I expect we will receive a formal call from the administration at that college sometime today. What did you find out?"

I sat across from her with my paper coffee cup from the Brew Shop and sipped the rich, hot French Vanilla mixture. I couldn't appear flummoxed. If you let this woman have the advantage you would never recover an equilibrium. Take a deep breath. What I wanted to say was that the purse idea was really pretty damn funny, but I knew better. "Unfortunately, not a lot. I spoke with the President of the KZ house, Winston Campbell, who assured me nothing like that had happened at the KZ house last night."

Emily sniped back, "And you believe him? Is he as big a prick as he seems? I heard that the Sheriff's department made an arrest." Emily often fired off sentences like staccato bursts from an automatic pistol. Once again I tried to regain control of the conversation.

"Officer Baker took a drunk and unconscious student into custody because his fraternity brothers served him up on the front porch, but I do not know if he was involved or not. Once he sobers up we will see if he can add anything."

Ms. Sellars just stared back. Pursing her lips she said, "Are you going to accept that? And what about at the Sigma Delta house?"

I was climbing back up the muddy slope. "Not much there either. The Sigma Delta house was almost deserted." I did not elect to share the "other meeting" information with her at this time.

She and I sat in high backed chairs so that she was facing the large arched window that looked out over the quadrangle in front of the administration and classroom buildings and across to the Student Union building. My back was to the window.

Diffused light painted the beveled glass of the window casting liquid sparkles on the floor. I swear I could not have discerned any difference between this room and a Don's office at Keeble College in Oxford. The sun was losing the fight to chase the clouds away and a dampness lay over everything.

Before she could reload, I noticed Emily was distracted and focused on the window, not on me. "What in the world?" she muttered. Her attention was so fixed that I had to turn so I could see. Refracted images around each pane's edge revealed three or four students running across the lawn slipping and sliding in the snow toward the administration building. Most of the runners wore black robes signifying their membership in the Honor Society, an award earned by the student's cumulative grade point average. The robes soared and flapped like a murder of disturbed crows and it was not long before the outer door of our office was breached. By this time both Emily and I were standing looking out the window at even more commotion across the Quad at the Student Union Building.

Out on the Quad students were flying around like leaves in the fall or wraiths in some moldy Victorian novel. Whatever had disturbed them had now caused them all to head back in the same direction toward the Student Union Building.

"Dean Mathews, come quick. Something has happened at the Student Union," a frantic student exclaimed as she rushed into our waiting area.

"Calm down, and slowly, please. What are you talking about?" I asked as I turned from the window and crossed to the door.

The breathless female student said "You must come see, Dean Mathews and Dean Sellars. I think he has been hurt, or worse."

"Or worse?" Emily said, her voice and one eyebrow rising.

"A student is chained in the back of a truck, and he is yelling and screaming. He has something all over him. It looks like corn flakes and feathers!" The other students who had accompanied her into my office were nodding in agreement.

Emily's eyes caught mine. We nodded and quickly left making our way down the hall to the exit steps gathering into our coats as we hurried. Nothing was spoken between us as we scrambled across the Quad lawn, crossed University Avenue, and there in the parking lot in front of the Student Union, we saw him. Or at least I think it was a him. It could have been a large duck.

In front of the Student Union building where a crowd was gathering was parked an open bed truck with the University logo on the side. I saw this same truck everyday almost, rumbling up and down University Avenue hauling wood from a downed tree. Tammy's husband, Leon, was often the driver. Chained and seated in the back of the truck, his arms outstretched in a Christ pose was a young man in boxer shorts who appeared covered in feathers and corn flakes. Around his neck hung a hand painted sign that said "I am a CHEATER." In the lower right hand side of the sign was a drawing of a knife covered in blood with the word "HONOR" below it. A couple of other students climbed up onto the flat bed and helped loosen the chains. The student yelled and screamed but his protests were growing weaker. He was shaking uncontrollably and I suspected hypothermia since the air temperature hovered around thirty-five degrees. His wild gyrations caused the other students to back away. No one wanted to hand him their coat since it was sure to be trashed by whatever concoction he was wearing. As the responsible adult, I jerked off my coat and put it around him watching as the cornflakes and feathers adhered to the inside of my coat as well. This wasn't going to improve my *Bob Newhart* image at all.

Students were milling around in shock. A few snapped cell phone pictures of this guy. I could hear the crowd murmuring. Some even pointed and giggled while others seemed genuinely concerned for the victim's situation. I couldn't imagine what had inspired this incident or what the sign meant. The image, however, was not one any of us would forget in a long time.

"Somebody call the hospital ambulance." I directed. "Does anyone know who this is? Is he a student?"

The victim, now muttering, was saying something about "torture", "white masks", and how he would get even. I heard the name "Savage" several times then he passed out. Someone in the crowd said, "I think that is Bob Anderson. He lives in McDonald Hall." Another student draped another blanket around Anderson's bare legs but he was shaking violently beneath the covers. Unable to hold the blanket Anderson slid over on one side and was unconscious in the flat bed, my jacket the only thing between his flesh and the cold metal of the truck. A gooey substance dripped off Mr. Anderson and collected in puddles on the greasy metal along with what I thought were corn flakes and down feathers.

The whole scene was surreal as the crowd formed around the truck necks craning to see what the fuss was about. I heard people gasp, and a few "Jesus Christ" or "Holy Shit" exclamations erupt. Whether or not it was appropriate to make such an utterance at a church school, it was pretty much exactly what I was thinking.

The ambulance jerked up to a stop and two students in EMT jump suits worked to place the victim on the stretcher but he was so slippery they almost dropped him like a wet squirming baby. In the process my jacket was liberally dosed with the mixture of feathers and cornflakes. Finally they had enough grip to get him onto the gurney and rushed him off to the small emergency room at the college hospital. The medical care wasn't great but considering our rural location it was all we had. Yogi's Sheriff's Department car pulled up at the same time and Yogi sprinted over to me.

"Jack, what's going on here?"

"Jesus, man, I don't have a clue. Emily Sellars and I were meeting about last night when students came bursting into my office saying that I had to get over here."

I had almost forgotten Emily so I glanced over to see that she was clearly pale. The feathered and flaked student had rattled her. I had never seen her at such a loss for words. Yogi said aloud to the growing mob of students, "I don't want anyone to leave. Anyone who saw anything or who knows anything should wait here and come into the Student Union where I can take statements." Few heeded his request and most wandered off. As did Emily. "I will catch up with you later." She mumbled as she glided into the crowd and away. I picked my jacket up off the ground and moaned at the new mixture plastered to the inside. This might be a throwaway. Luckily, I had an old Cabella's jacket that would work, and at least I wouldn't look like the handyman any longer.

The students still circling around the Union seemed to be energized by what they had seen. Some appeared shocked while others joked and laughed. The casual flow of students between classes moving from this point to that had been interrupted by the spectacle of Mr. Anderson with his decorated torso. It was not something any of them had ever witnessed, or me either. Whoever had done this was bold, and had carefully planned the entire operation. How we would ever solve this mystery would depend a lot upon luck and whether some fine detail had been overlooked in the cover up process. I was confident if such a detail had been missed, Yogi would ferret it out.

CHAPTER FIVE

While Yogi took statements in the Student Union, I speed walked the mile out to the university hospital. The sun was still hidden but the snow had slowed clouds sporadically spitting out the last of their moisture. Air was what I needed and a little time to assimilate all that had happened in the last 24 hours. After college I had continued to run cross country, as I had done as a student, and the walk to the hospital ER was restorative. I had never seen anything like that chained and befeathered student before. Fraternity "hell week" and the hazing of freshmen had passed into memory, myth and legend and was gone from student life at the University, or at least so I thought. Those activities were subject to serious sanctions on campus at this point including expulsion. Whoever had been involved may have felt they would not be apprehended and if they were caught, thought they would be insulated from the consequences. This incident seemed an odd throwback to some prehistoric time when the school had been an exclusively male institution and was not as "sensitive" as it had now become. Back then no one thought twice when pledges ate dog food sandwiches, wore raw liver in their underwear, slugged down Lydia Pinkham's special potion for hot flashes, or had a too short string attached on one end to a pencil and on the other to their pecker as they procured the autograph of upperclassmen. The older boys were only too willing to oblige since the string would need to be yanked taught in order to reach a writing pad. Ah, the good old days.

At the ER nurse's desk I identified myself and said I thought the student's name was Bob Anderson. I had already called my office to get the contact information for his family.

"That's a help. After all, since he showed up in his boxer shorts there wasn't much place for identification." Said the attending nurse who was a lumpy red-haired battle axe of a woman. It was clear she ran the place.

"How is he doing?" I asked.

"Not well. I cannot tell you much, HIPPA you know, but since his parents are not here, I will tell you that he is in for a rough time. Exposure, shock, who knows what else when we get all that stuff off of him. We can't tell if he has any other injuries."

I asked, "Could you tell what was all over him?"

"Best I can say, feathers from a down pillow and cornflakes, held on by molasses." The tag on her uniform said "Garland".

"Nurse Garland, is he awake?" I asked.

"We have him sedated. It will be awhile before he will be able to talk with anyone," she responded dismissing me with nothing more than a look returning to her paperwork.

I turned when I heard the whoosh of the automatic emergency room doors to see a female student hustling into the ER. She had been crying and was clearly still distraught. "Where is he? Where is Bob?" She cried.

I put my arm around her shoulders and guided her over to the hospital issue plastic sofas in the waiting area. "Miss ?..."

"Autumn Starr..." she whispered.

"Miss Starr, do you know Mr. Anderson, if that's his name?" I asked all the while trying to calm her. She continued sobbing and shaking. It occurred to me I might have some connection to this girl. The voice I had heard before? "Did you by any chance call my home last night?" I asked. Was I now meeting caller number 2?

Miss Autumn Starr was wearing a down jacket over a sweatshirt and jeans. Her hair was mostly blonde, but with black and purple sections. Her lipstick, eye gloss and nail polish all signaled her as a devote of the Gothic look, not a common look on this campus. Co-eds here could not go home and face their parents looking like this. Yet, a small group of bright but unconventional students, who probably smoked most of the pot on campus, hung together in a close knit group. They were known as the "gypsies". I figured Autumn Starr as part of this group, perhaps Anderson as well. I had received a quick tutorial on the gypsies from Emily Sellars after I moved into the office.

"Like most college campuses these days, we have our share of fruits and nuts," Emily had said. "You'll see soon enough, but our group call themselves the "Gypsies". You will be able to pick them out from the clothing, the hair, and the makeup. Sometimes there's an abundance of piercings. One thing you can count on is that in their attempt to be "unconventional" they become much more homogenous with each other. Many of the group are very bright, high achieving test scores and academic credentials. There are even a few who hang around this group and who do not adopt the appearance, so they are more difficult to pick out. All in all, I think they are pretty harmless, although they do not participate much in the social life of fraternities and sororities, or in student government. The last place you would find a gypsy is on an athletic team, unless its on the cross country team, and those guys are nuts anyway."

I could have taken issue with Emily at the time since I had been on the cross-country team in my day and didn't have a pony tail even then, but I got her point. There had to be something unhinged about running until you puked.

The girl next to me on the plastic sofa grew quiet. After a moment she said "Yes, I called you last night. I did not know what to do. I am Bob's friend, his girlfriend."

"Please tell me what happened last night," I prompted, in my best empathetic tone, one that I might someday use to persuade a jury to trust me.

"Bob and I had agreed to meet in his dorm room around 8 o'clock last night. He lives in

McDonald and I am in Emerson, next door." Eight o'clock was approximately the same time I was approaching the KZ house in the snow storm but I hadn't seen anything. McDonald and Emerson were older dorms in the opposite direction near the south side of campus.

"Bob was late. He said that on the way to his dorm after dinner, he was walking down University Avenue when this other student got in his face. They got into an argument over a letter Bob had written to the *Onion*. Bob said the guy was a real asshole." Autumn continued.

"I haven't seen the latest *Onion* yet, why don't you tell me about the letter." I wanted her to fill in as many details as she could as Harry Bosch would have recommended.

"Well, you see, we do not think much of the school's Honor Code." She looked up at me." Most of the students are rich hypocrites, who don't care about the important things. So..." she sniffled, "Bob decided to get in their face so he wrote a letter to the Editor of the *Onion.*" Autumn got quiet again. Allowing her to slow the sobbing, I watched as she wrenched one hand over the other nervously as if to wash something off.

I asked, "And what did the letter to the editor say?" This next part was hard to pull out of her. She clearly felt she had to defend Bob Anderson.

"Bob is very smart," she started. "He has read a lot of philosophy and is a deep thinker. He hates, I mean he really hates hypocrites. He talks about how religion is hypocritical, the church is hypocritical, all these Bishops and Trustees, and all of it is just so hypocritical…" Her voice trailed off. I did not think it productive to debate her just at this time so I encouraged her to run with the line like a big cutthroat.

"Bob was pissed and he was yelling. I tried to calm him down, and when that didn't work I lit a joint for him…" She gulped and quickly realized she probably should not have said that to a school official like me.

"It's ok Autumn, I am only here to find out what happened. Please go on." I encouraged.

"We smoked a little and Bob began to settle down. We talked about his letter. In the letter Bob said he had cheated on every exam he had taken. That the Honor Code was a joke, the University was a joke, and he had seen others cheating on exams," Autumn had settled into a rhythm now and had begun to open up. Anderson was a junior so that means he had cheated on maybe fifteen exams in two and a half years. I was having a hard time believing someone could pull that off without anyone detecting the scheme.

"Who did he meet on the way back to the dorm?" I asked.

"Bob, said it was Tom Savage." Autumn offered.

I said "Do you mean the Editor of the *Onion*?"
I considered Tom Savage to be very upstanding. He
was a good student, and a member of the Discipline
Committee, an elected committee run by students to
deal with unacceptable behavior within the student
body. They actually had the power to expel another
student. Personally, I couldn't see Savage having a
part in a tar and feather operation.

"Yes. Bob said they were face to face almost
spitting on each other. Savage was defending the
Honor Code and Bob said he stood by his letter.
The Code was all a joke."

"Was that the end of it? Nobody pushed or
threw any punches or anything, did they?" I asked.
Since Tom Savage was very cerebral and not much
of a physical guy, I would have been shocked if he
had initiated a fight. If Anderson was going back to
his dorm that would explain his direction of travel
on the opposite side of the Avenue than I had been
walking.

Autumn paused and said "Not then, anyway.
But later…"

"Tell me about later, Autumn." I was coaxing
every word out of her like pulling eye teeth.

A flurry of activity electrified the nurse's
station. Alarms were going off, the few nurses on
duty were running down the hallway. Autumn and I
were distracted, and we both looked around. I said
"Please tell me about later".

She looked back at me. "Later, after our second joint, the door to Bob's room busted open. Three or four guys wearing white hoods jumped in and grabbed him. They put a black hood over his head and one of them had a rope they wrapped around his neck and around his arms. I was screaming, it was horrible." Autumn was really getting worked up this time. Her words were broken and jumpy. I was getting distracted by her hands-one over the other, washing, washing.

"Tell me about the rope, Autumn."

"I think…I think it had a loop at one end. You know, like a hangman's rope."

"Is that what they put around his neck?" I questioned incredulously.

"Yes. Bob was fighting and kicking and yelling but these guys were strong and big. I tried to grab one of them but he pushed me away and I fell against the sofa. I must have hit my head and passed out, because when I came to, it was much later and they were gone. That's when I tried to call you. When you weren't there, I saw blood on the floor and it all flashed in front of me again. I screamed. I guess I passed out again. I woke a little while ago and when I got to the Student Union, someone told me Bob had been hurt."

"Could you tell who any of the attackers were? Could you give me any descriptions? White guys or black guys?"

She thought a moment and said, "No, I don't remember anything like that. It was all too fast and crazy. But Bob was so mad at Tom Savage, and he at Bob, it wouldn't surprise me that he had something to do with it."

The alarms that had been ripping the air apart in the ER grew eerily silent. Autumn and I sat there, catching our breaths and trying to sort through this cacophony of information. My head hurt, and I couldn't imagine why Bob Anderson had been attacked. Why had he been covered in feathers and chained in a truck with the sign around his neck? I couldn't believe Tom Savage would have anything to do with it, but perhaps he did. That confrontation and shouting contest coming so quickly before the later attack may not have been a coincidence. What were we coming to, and why in the hell didn't I take that job with that big city law firm or even Wyoming?

Nurse Garland approached us with a determined measured stride. She motioned for me to join her at the station with a gesture from her left hand. I patted Autumn on the shoulder and told her I would be right back. In a rehearsed voice, I knew she had used before, Nurse Garland said, "I am so sorry. But we really need that boy's parents now. I am afraid Mr. Anderson has slipped into a coma. He was in cardiac arrest there for a moment. The shock and exposure were too much."

Bob Anderson was seriously hurt. Holy shit.

CHAPTER SIX

"YOGI"

My friend, Jack Mathews, left to go to the hospital with the vic, which is what we in police work call, the "victim". Kids were scattering everywhere after the ambulance left. In my best policeman's voice, I said "Please, remain calm. I need to take a statement from everyone who saw anything or knows anything that would assist in the investigation. I will set up at a table in the Union and I would ask that you come in one at a time and tell me what happened."

I had grabbed my notebook from my patrol car and sat down at a round table in the far corner of the Student Union. This was the before and after class gathering place for students and faculty. The building, also of native sandstone had been the focus of social life, outside the dining hall and frat houses, for forty years. The Union had an old fashioned soda counter where you could order soft drinks, coffee, shakes and French fries. The fries quickly became a communal plate with multiple sets of fingers like piranha tearing into the potatoes. Defensively, some quickly smothered the fries with mustard to deter the hungry fish.

After taking my seat and removing my Smokey the Bear hat, I motioned for the first student to join me. His name was Steve Dorfman.

"Mr. Dorfman, did you see what happened here?" I questioned. Dorfman was tall with unruly blonde hair.

"Yes, sir. I was sitting at that table over there by the big window when the truck pulled up out front. I thought that was odd since those school maintenance trucks do not park in this area. There's no reason for them to. When the truck stopped someone wearing a white hood jumped out of the cab and began running back down University Avenue."

"Could you tell anything about the runner?"

"Only that he was fast. Fast, I mean, like a track guy." Dorfman added.

I asked, "Did you see Mr. Anderson at that point?"

"Not at first. I saw the runner, and the truck was still running. Its muffler was loud, maybe broken off. But, then I saw this guy in the back yelling. Then people started to come around. I got up and went outside. Somebody turned the truck off."

"Did you happen to know Mr. Anderson? " I pressed.

Dorfman said "I knew who he was but until I got outside I couldn't be sure. He was a mess, Kinda funny in a way."

"Funny?" I asked. "What did you think was funny?"

"Well, to see a guy covered in feathers and cornflakes. I mean, you don't see that every day." Dorfman added.

I decided to pursue this further, "Have you ever seen it before? I mean someone covered in feathers and cornflakes?"

Dorfman's alarm system went off and he became a little less cooperative. "Have you, Mr. Dorfman?"

"During my freshman year, one of the football team freshman players came back to the dorm after Hell Week covered in cornflakes. He dropped his clothes in the hall and washed it off in the shower. The cornflakes stopped up the shower for days, and then someone set fire to his clothes in the hall." Dorfman still found humor in all this.

"Anything else you can tell me Mr. Dorfman?"

"Only that Bob Anderson was one of the gypsies. Have you heard of them?" I allowed that I had not.

"Yeah, a real gypsy, maybe their leader. Certainly a weirdo." Dorfman added.

"A Gypsy?" I asked.

"Yeah, that's what people call them. You know, non-conformists, generally weird."

I encouraged him to go on.

"Some say their goal is to tear down everything the school stands for. You saw Anderson's letter to the editor in the *Purple* ? The guy really flaunts the Honor Code. Says he cheats and gets away with it and so does everybody else. And, they protest everything. They hate Republicans, cops are pigs, priests are pedophiles, and it goes on and on."

"I was not aware of such a group here." I commented.

"Check on Anderson. I hear the Gypsies even do black masses underneath the Chapel."

Dorfman had my attention when someone yelled, "Hey Dorf, we gotta go. Tell Barney Fife you'll talk to him later." Mr. Dorfman excused himself and jogged out.

My interlude with Dorfman had taken so long the other students had now scattered. I felt like I was herding cats. My cell phone buzzed, it was Jack Mathews.

"Yogi?"

"Yeah, Jack."

"You aren't going to believe this, but our little cornflakes and feathers just got worse."

"What", I asked. "What did you say?"

Jack came back, "Anderson just went into a coma from the shock and exposure."

I asked, "Where are you?"

"Still wrapping it up at the ER." Jack said.

"I'll pick you up in two." I left on a run to my patrol car and the only thing I could think of was how in the hell did this happen? Things had gotten serious.

CHAPTER SEVEN

"Jack"

I stood outside the ER in a drifting breeze that always seemed to climb up one side of the Mountain and then roll down the other. This time of year it brought a low hanging fog that often obscured the tops of the trees and buildings on campus. There were even times when that fog would freeze and encircle entire tree branches creating what seemed to be an imaginary glistening landscape of ice. Tammy called it a "hoar" frost. When that happened our campus seemed even more isolated and frozen in time.

As I waited for Yogi I was literally and figuratively ensnared in a white out zone. As much as I tried to reconcile what was happening I was having a very hard time organizing what I knew. How had things spiraled out of control so quickly? Yesterday, I was on route to tackle the problem of a turd in a purse, and now a student was near death. Suddenly, one of my students was very ill and poop in a purse seemed pretty insignificant. I knew it would not be long before word about Anderson blew all over the campus like the mountain climbing fog. I had so much to do but where should I start? My office was likely a war zone with several people waiting for me to report in and provide reliable information. As much as I wanted to sidestep that melee, I could not avoid it. I owed it to the student's family to call as well as to get the President up to speed. Then there was the obvious need to coordinate the school's investigation and response.

As promised, Yogi pulled up in front and I climbed into his patrol car. Yogi had on his winter police gear and gloves. I didn't see how he could comfortably sit and drive with the bulky weapons belt on but I figured that was his problem.

"I called into dispatch and they will call in some forensic assistance out of Chattanooga. May take a little while. You know Jack you need to ditch that hat, makes you look like the maintenance guy on *Bob Newhart*."

Almost in a daze I said, "Thanks a lot for the clothing advice, Smokey. Let's go to my office. There are calls I need to make and we need to discuss how I can help you with the investigation." My personal appearance was the least of my troubles at that point.

The patrol car tires bit into the crusty ice and snow and pulled away slowly from the ER towards the administration building and my office. In a matter of minutes we were curbside on University Avenue. The pursuing fog masked the sun creating a boding sense of further drama. The campus was strangely quiet. Yogi and I took the steps two at a time up to my second floor offices. On the way he said, "Remember the story of the guys who brought a cow up these steps and let it spend the night crapping in the hall and all over the classrooms?" Yogi was fascinated with the history of this place.

"And how they found that a cow will not go down a set of stairs so they had to bring in a crane to get it out?" I smiled. It was a great tale but at the moment even Yogi's stories weren't taking anything off the edge of my anxiety.

At the door to the joint offices I shared with Emily Sellars a few students sat around on the pew like benches. I acknowledged them but did not hesitate to get inside my chambers without engaging them in conversation. Officer Baker followed. After we said hello to Ms. Algood I told Tammy to get the President on the line and to set up a meeting with the Editor of the *Purple* and the student President of the Honor Council for 3 o'clock. I also asked her to get me the phone number for the parents of Mr. Anderson.

To my last request, Tammy replied, "They have already called and should be here late tonight. I think they are driving in from Louisville. You have a meeting set with them for 10 am tomorrow."

"Ok, Thanks. I need to see Mr. Anderson's student file."

There was no sign that Ms. Sellars had returned to her office. Yogi and I sat at the round table in one corner of my office. Ms. Algood shut my door and left as soon as she dropped the Robert Anderson file on the table.

As I rubbed my eyes and temples, Yogi started, "Jack, I am going to need some help on this case. We don't have the resources in our sheriff's department to properly investigate a situation like this. I am the only true detective, and we only have one crime scene specialist. I do not want to make anything worse for you or the school, but I need to call the TBI."

"The FBI?" I muttered looking up at him through bloodshot eyes.

"No, the TBI, Tennessee Bureau of Investigation." I had apparently not heard him correctly. "I have a friend who is an agent there. Guy I was at the Academy with. Since they are based in Nashville, I should be able to have them here tomorrow. Now, I need to know this boy's dorm room so I can begin to secure a crime scene." Yogi said.

I picked up the thin file with the name Robert G. Anderson on the side tab. I flipped to the top sheet and said, "Anderson's room is McDonald Hall, Room 300. That is the only room on the third floor. McDonald is an older dorm about two blocks down from the Student Union. The third floor dorm room is the gabled peak you see from the front of the street. This says he did not have a roommate." I knew that room. It had been mine once.

Yogi wrote this information in his notepad and stood to go. He said, "I am really sorry Jack. I need to secure his room and call my CSI tech. Tomorrow I am sure I will need to start talking with more students who may have seen something. I heard you ask to meet with two students in a little while, the Honor Council President and the editor of the *Purple* ?"

" Yes, I know both of those young men. I think they are good guys, and because of their positions on campus, they are likely to have heard much more than either of us about what really happened. I will update you after that meeting but I think it is best I not have a police officer present at this initial meeting."

Yogi said he understood and left. That was when Ms. Allgood stuck her head in and said the President was on line one. Here we go. The President was a portly soul in his mid-sixties. Behind his back some of the faculty referred to him as *Rumpole*. But, it was his eyebrows that always distracted me. The way they curled and stretched across his square forehead with no break over his nose resembled the brow of a Neanderthal. His booming voice suggested a hellfire and damnation sermon on a rock in a pasture next to some Scottish mountain.

"Jack, what in God's name is going on?" President Duncan Callicott demanded. As the president of the school he was responsible only to the Board of Trustees. He had served for thirty years and his bushy grey eyebrows and flowing mane of white hair made an imposing presentation, even when you were talking with him over the phone because his voice was so unique his image immediately flashed before your eyes. I could see him leaning way back in his leather desk chair, the phone up to one ear, a cigar in his other hand and a half full glass of Jack Black on his desk. It was as if you were being scolded by James Earl Jones with a Virginia Tidewater accent. "Spit it out, boy. What is going on?"

I was much more than a "boy", and I was certainly not his "boy", but then again he had hired me into this job and he was the boss. "Sir, we have had an unfortunate incident where a student was apparently kidnapped and made the butt of a joke on account of statements he made about the Honor Code. The student was left in front of the Student Union this morning covered with feathers and cornflakes. Presently, he is in serious condition at the hospital." There, I said it, no sugarcoating that.

Now,the Prez roared, "How sick is he? Are you telling me someone kidnapped and almost killed one of our students? Who did such a thing? Have you contacted the police?"

I was trying to keep up with the barrage of questions, "Sir, we don't know who just yet. All this happened within the past few hours. The Sheriff's department is on the scene and I am interviewing a couple of student leaders in the next few minutes. I will update you immediately as soon as I know something else."

"What was the boy's name?" President Callicott asked.

I replied, "Robert Anderson. He is from the Louisville area."

"There is something familiar about that name."
"Anderson. Anderson" the President repeated. "I don't have to tell you what this can do to our enrollment and yes, our endowment as well. Well, I expect to be the first you call the minute you learn anything else."

"Yes, Sir" I said after he had hung up. I realized my knuckles were white from gripping the phone. I laid the receiver down and took a deep breath. With my hands on my temples I thought hang in there, just hang in there.

CHAPTER EIGHT

Special Agent Rockford "Rockie" Bradley of the TBI was assigned to assist the Sequoyah County Sheriff's department investigation of the student assault. SA Bradley was a stout fellow with trunk like thighs, bulging arms, and a moderately flat stomach to match. He loved his designation of "Special" Agent of the TBI. In fact all law enforcement officers of the TBI below the rank of Sergeant were special agents. Nonetheless, such designation appropriately described his talents and mission, at least in his own mind. One big plus was that he got to carry a Beretta PX4 with a five inch barrel and a .32 caliber throw down in his ankle holster. He was quick with a broad grin and well liked among other officers.

SA Bradley drove an unmarked black "muscle" car that was at least 15 years old, it having been acquired by the TBI in a recent drug enforcement action. He knew little of our University or Sequoyah County since he had lived in and around Nashville for the past 35 years. The TBI Captain who had assigned him to the case told him to provide whatever assistance the Sequoyah County Sheriff needed and to file a report every morning on line with the Captain's email.

In two hours SA Bradley had reached the office of Sheriff Buford Baker in the small town of Northwoods which had been described to him as a wide spot in the road. Climbing the steps to the Sheriff's Office which also served as the county jail he noticed second floor brick windows with iron bars. There didn't seem to be any glass on those windows. Odd he thought. He hoped they didn't keep prisoners in there exposed to this kind of weather. After the initial introductions, he was briefed by Deputy Yogi Baker on the facts as they were known one day after the victim's assault. Deputy Baker seemed like an ok guy to him in an Andy Griffith kind of way. Local law enforcement was about as skeptical of TBI agents as they were of FBI stiff backed suited officers who rolled up on locals and took command of everything. Yogi however, sensed something different about Special Agent Bradley and thought they could work together. They had met a few years earlier at the police academy in Nashville. The Sheriff, Buford Baker, just sat there staring a hole in SA Bradley.

" Around 3:00 pm yesterday I went to the vic's dorm room and secured the area with crime tape." Officer Baker allowed. "The first thing I noticed was that the room had been completely torn apart. These dorm rooms are pretty sparse to begin with but someone had removed all the bed sheets, broken the furniture and had sliced up the mattresses. Not sure what they were looking for." Buford adjusted himself in his chair but still had not spoken.

"This happened how long after the student was found on campus?" asked SA Bradley.

Baker responded, "Only a couple of hours."

"That seems strange. Do you think the kidnapping and the room search are related?" Bradley queried.

"No way to tell at this point. We could not see that anything was missing. There were fingerprints all over everywhere but we are not likely to find a match. Students are not fingerprinted, and usually have no criminal record when they enroll at the school."

SA Bradley asked more, "Have you interviewed other residents of that dorm?"

"Not yet," Baker said with some frustration, "You could be of great assistance with that."

"Glad to help. Tell me where I can get a list of the residents of that dorm and I will start right away."

A list of the residents had been faxed to Deputy Baker by Dean Mathews's office so Baker made a copy and handed one to SA Bradley.

"You will keep me posted as to everything you discover won't you Agent Bradley?" Buford asked.

"For sure, Sheriff," Bradley acknowledged.

After receiving directions to the residence hall, SA Bradley fired up his car and drove up the mountain into the growing fog bank.

When Bradley was gone Buford pulled Yogi aside and said, "Yogi, I want to be kept informed about everything you find in this investigation, and whatever that Agent comes up with. Play it by the book and log in all evidence to Pete." Pete was the keeper of the evidence room at the jail.

"Understand?" Buford asked.

"Got it, Chief," Yogi said.

CHAPTER NINE

A meeting of the gypsies was called for the basement dorm room of Woody German at 10 pm on the evening Bob Anderson had been taken to the hospital. Fifteen gypsies attended completely filling every square inch of available floor space with standing room only on the edges as late comers were forced to lean against the block walls. Anderson had been their leader, almost prophet-like. Although the gypsies thought of themselves as non-conformists and free thinkers, they reacted like a herd of swallows changing direction frequently. Despite their vows of non-conformity most gypsies were easily identifiable by their clothing, makeup and hair styles. A pale sweetness of incense and marijuana permeated the air. Everyone was talking nervously in muted voices when Woody stood up and began:

" Thank you all for coming. Please, please keep it down. At this point we need to assume the worst and watch out for each other. I don't know what is going on, but this is bad. Someone or some group really roughed up Bob. What I have been able to find out is that on Sunday night Bob was confronted on University Avenue by Tom Savage, the *Purple* editor. Later, four hooded guys snatched him from his room and knocked out Autumn." In the corner, Autumn was nodding her head. A girl squatting on the floor next to Autumn reached over and patted her arm. "The next morning he was dropped off in front of the Union in a flat bed truck chained down with a sign around his neck and covered with feathers and cornflakes. From there he was moved to the ER at the hospital where he is now in a coma." The group murmur rose.

"Cool it guys." Woody admonished. "We have got to figure some stuff out. Has anyone been to his room?" No one had thought to look.

"We'll check on that later." Woody went on, "Has anyone heard anything, seen anything? We need to know what happened to Bob after he was grabbed."

One of the girls named Veggie Barnes said," at dinner the other night there was a lot of laughing and joking going on between the KZ and Sigma Delta tables. I was working the dining hall that night at their tables. I heard pieces of conversation about the "Plan" and how they needed to show up near mid-night at the Cabin." The main dining hall still served food family style with student waiters working for their room and board who brought trays of food to each table and then cleaned up the mess when it was over. The worst tables to serve were where the football team ate especially on fried chicken night when the center of the table became a bone yard resembling the carcass of a dinosaur before the meal finished.

Woody asked," What Cabin? Do you mean the Forestry Cabin at the edge of the mountain?"

"It's the only one I know" Veggie said. "I also heard someone mention everything was set up with the truck." People started to look around.

One of the other gypsies said " What if the jocks grabbed Bob on account of his letter?"

Another one said, "that newspaper guy, Savage, could have been in on it. Sounds like he threatened Bob just before he was taken."

Woody asked, "Veggie, do you know who was at those tables? Could you identify them?"

"I don't know. Maybe with a picture book."

"The point is, what are we going to do about it?" another gypsy said.

"We have to get even. We can't just take this. This is war," someone said and Woody realized he was close to losing control. Like the others he was mad but knew he had to react cautiously and smart.

Again Woody said, "Whoa guys. These jocks are all big guys, we do not want a one on one with any of them. We need to respond but only with tactical strikes."

Henry Chen, acknowledged as the brightest campus computer geek, spoke up. Henry was a tall thin Asian fellow. His skills with the computer were legendary. "I can flunk all of them in enough courses by hacking into the university computer system to make the entire basketball team ineligible and they can kiss spring football practice goodbye."

Laughter and whoops broke out at the thought. "Get em Chensky" someone said. Now they were cooking, Woody thought.

"We need them to feel some heat," said Joey Pressley. "What if their girlfriends got anonymous phone calls or emails? Let's see if we can't rattle their cages a bit. Henry can you get me cell numbers?"

"Sure" Henry said, "I just need names."

Woody then assigned three of the gypsies to get names of all the KZ's and Sigma Deltas since they had the largest number of jocks as members, and the names of their girlfriends who could be identified. Social media sites already posted party weekend photographs and facial recognition software could quickly identify enough to get them started.

Someone else said, "But what about other jocks? We don't even know if we are after the right group."

Woody said "We have to start somewhere. Everybody see what you can find out. We will meet here again tomorrow night. Same time. Don't start anything yet. When we respond, it needs to be good. And, keep your mouth shut."

Henry lingered after the others left. All his life he had been waiting to get back at big tough athletes who had picked on him since junior high. Now, he could sense the opportunity was near and it was exciting.

"Woody, it's not enough just to hassle the jocks. We need to make a statement that puts gypsies on the map. A move that no one will forget. I am thinking we need to take over the university's server not just fuck with it a little bit," Henry mused.

"You can do that?" asked Woody.

"That part is a piece of cake, but I will need to get into the computer lab tonight. I will see if I can get access to work on a project late. Tomorrow will be a new day for the university." Henry was on a roll now.

Woody said "Henry can you do this without getting into trouble? What if they catch you?"

"Not to worry. There is no one here capable of tracking me. Even though I will hack into the system from within, it will appear as if I am located in Eastern Europe," said Henry.

Woody had bought into the moment. A plan was sparking in his head. As a film major, Woody loved old black and white classics, especially the horror movies of the 1930's. His mind was whirring like a 16 mm projector. "Henry, I have an idea…"

CHAPTER TEN

I asked Tammy to open a special file named "Anderson Investigation". I would later change the name. At 3 pm sharp both Tom Savage and Clendon Crawford, President of the Honor Council, were led into my office by Ms. Allgood.

We sat around my circular table where she had set out bottles of water and I began,

"Gentlemen, as you know, earlier today Bob Anderson was left chained and humiliated in the back of a flat bed truck in front of the Student Union just as classes changed. What you may not know is that a few hours ago he slipped into a coma at University Hospital."

Both Savage and Crawford started talking at once. I raised both hands, palms out and said, "I have called you here to assist me in dealing with this unpleasant turn of events. Mr. Savage, before I go any further, it is my understanding you had a confrontation with Mr. Anderson on University Avenue at approximately 8 pm on Sunday night. I need to know all about that meeting."

Savage was bright and glib, his words measured and paced. Mr. Crawford was clearly in the dark about that encounter between Savage and Anderson and just stared with his mouth open. "Yes, sir. We published the new edition of the *Purple* at dinner on Saturday. It is our policy to print all letters to the editor even though we may disagree with the content or find it offensive, just so long as it is not pornographic. By agreement with the University we draw the line at obscenity. Mr. Anderson submitted a letter indicating the Honor Code was a joke, and that he and others had cheated on exams on a regular basis. I took offense at his attitude and his letter, so when I accidentally encountered him that night we had words."

I asked, "Can you remember exactly what was said?"

"Yes, sir, quite clearly." Savage responded. "Do you want to know what I said, exactly?"

"Of course," I said.

Savage wetted his lips and said, "I told him he was a fucking weirdo and little shit ball. And, that if he thought so little of the school he should just leave. Then I told him someone should jerk a half hitch in his ass." Savage stopped realizing what he had just said, then continued, "Anderson just laughed at me and said he would not let something as archaic as the Honor Code interfere with him."

"Do you know what he meant by that?" I asked watching his face closely. I recalled that Anderson had said the name "Savage" several times before he passed out.

"No sir. It was cold. I said my piece, he said his and we parted. I didn't see him again. Are you serious, he is in bad shape?" Savage asked.

"I am afraid so, and you appear to have been

one of the last people to see him," I said still focused on his reaction as I tried to determine if he was telling me the truth or holding something back.

At this point, Clendon Crawford joined in "Dean Mathews, we have heard this kind of trash from a certain element before. There are always those who do not buy into the system. Who do not understand what makes this school special."

I responded looking away from Savage to Mr. Crawford "Yes, but this is obviously more serious now. A student is hurt, and that same student publically claimed he and others cheated on exams at this school. As Dean it is my responsibility to investigate the cheating claims and assist the authorities with their investigation of the assault. I have called you in because I think you are both outstanding and principled students. You each have a position of respect and authority on campus, and quite frankly you are closer to the ebb and flow of the student body than I as an administrator can ever be. I need you to help serve as my eyes and ears, but also to help control to the extent we can the dissemination of information about this matter."

Mr. Savage coughed, "Dean Mathews, are you asking the *Purple* to hold back or censor itself?"

"Nothing of the sort, " I answered , "but I do expect cooperation and responsibility on your part. I am sure you realize the budget for the *Purple* runs through this office?"

My insinuation was not lost on him as Tom

Savage continued:

"Sir, I fully understand, but we must honestly report the news." Savage objected.

"I will not ask you to do anything unethical or untruthful, but we need to get out in front of this story, for the good of the University." I said.

"How can I help?" asked Savage.

"Good. What I need is for you to do is to crank out a short one page special edition of the *Purple* to report on Mr. Anderson's abduction with some personal interest information about him as a student. No editorializing at this point. We need everyone to settle down and not completely disrupt this campus for the balance of this semester. Perhaps your article could ask anyone with information to contact the paper."

Savage was still looking at me as if he wasn't sure he could trust me. Finally, he said "I assume you will want to review the copy before we go to press."

I retorted "Do you think I need to Mr. Savage? Haven't I made myself clear?"

"I understand." He said.

"Where do I fit in Dean Mathews" asked Clendon Crawford. Where Mr. Savage had the reporter's appetite for controversy and the "low deeds of the higher ups", Mr. Crawford exuded an air of self-control and confidence. As Chairman of the Honor Council, he had been elected twice by the student body without opposition. His character could not have been more genuine or his reputation any stronger. I needed him to spearhead my investigation. Before we parted today each of these young men would know that I needed them for very different operations.

"Mr. Crawford, the Honor Code is, I believe, at the heart of this matter. Mr. Anderson threw down the gauntlet. He has challenged the very soul of what we stand for. I went to school here and thousands of students before me have all pledged oath to the Honor Code. It is the fabric of community we can all agree upon. It is a major part of our social contract. We cannot let it be tarnished. Mr. Anderson and perhaps others do not agree with that position, and as such, have placed themselves outside our community. But, if he was kidnapped and humiliated, perhaps even tortured by other students, we need to know that, because their action is also a breach of our social order. As President of the Honor Council I want you to lead the University's investigation into this event. I want you to bring witnesses before the Council and grill them. I want to know the truth. The University body must know what and why this has happened. Pull no punches, but be confidential in what you learn. I want daily reports, but only to me. You are not to share your data with Mr. Savage."

Each of them stared at me. "I mean it gentlemen. Mr. Savage your job is to report the facts and to do what you can to find the pulse of the student community here. You have a creative bunch of reporters, especially that guy, what's his name, Wombat? But before you write one word, you check with me. I will give you considerable leeway, but if you cross me or become a problem, I will shut you down quicker than Pepto Bismal. Mr. Crawford, you are to be the visible investigating arm of this school as far as the students are concerned. Develop the facts, report them to me, and me only. I am serious as a heart attack with both of you. There will be local and state police on scene shortly. We will cooperate with them, but I do not want to hear something bad from them before I hear it from you."

Mr. Crawford appealed, "Dean Mathews, I think you know we will do our best, but I want you to understand we are both seniors and in less than a month we will be sitting for our final exams and oral comprehensive exams in our majors. I don't think there is time to do what you ask us to do, and still graduate." Mr. Savage was nodding.

"I want daily reports from each of you on my personal email, that's jmathews@rocket.com. Got it?" Both nodded.

"Then, I suggest you get started, and find the time." I had supercharged and then let the air out of the room all at the same time. As they left I was thinking, boys I hate to do this to you but we are in for a ride.

CHAPTER ELEVEN

The skills of Henry Chen enabled the gypsies to develop information on their adversaries with incredible speed. Within a few hours he had accessed the Registrar's Office and had cell numbers and email addresses for each member of the KZ and Sigma Delta fraternity houses. Girl friend information was harder to come by and was more incomplete. He was forced to hack into the University email server to track emails from some of the more prominent members of those fraternities. This was an easy task since he had assisted the University IT department to set up email accounts. He still had the password list. Some of the emails he captured were quite juicy. He made a mental note to return to them later. Once he had secured a half dozen email accounts for female students who regularly emailed and texted with junior and senior KZ and Sigma Delta members, he was ready for tonight's meeting. In addition, he had run facial recognition on the party weekend photos that were already appearing on Facebook sites for the KZ's and Sigma Deltas to confirm the identity of some of the targets.

Woody German presided once again over the second planning meeting of the gypsies. His basement dorm room lent itself to some privacy since there were no jocks residing on this floor of the dorm. "Ok, let's settle down. We have been thinking about this, and are going to call our war plan "Operation Jock Itch." A quiet laughter spread. " Some of you may have seen the symbol on the sign around Bob's neck. It was a knife dripping red with blood."

"The Red Dagger" someone said.

"Does anyone know what the Red Dagger is?" Again, from the back someone said, "it is a secret society of campus jocks, football players, basketball and baseball players and track guys, but mostly football. It has been around for awhile and somehow a former student, Braxton Johnson was involved." Everyone above the freshman level remembered Braxton since he had been the star of a nearly non-existent football team only a year or so ago. Braxton had a low center of gravity and moved like a bowling ball through the opposing lines whether he was starting at fullback or as a nose guard. Braxton had no problem running into brick walls. He was well liked and an easily recognizable figure on campus while he was a student.

Woody asked, "How do you know so much about the Red Dagger?"

"Because Johnson was my suite-mate my freshman year. I heard all about it."

"And…" Woody prompted.

"It was created by a few guys who believed the school had lost its way and was wrong about tolerating so much political correctness. They couldn't believe what the school was turning into. Mostly though, these guys just drank a bunch of beer and talked big about what a fine day it was to whoop somebody's ass."

Woody said, "Braxton Johnson graduated last year and I hear he is in basic training at the Marine Corps base at Quantico. He couldn't be involved."

"Ah, but you may be wrong." Everyone was now looking at the speaker sitting in the shadows of the dorm room. "There is a lot of chatter about the Red Dagger at dinner and anytime you go to the gym." Finally, Woody was able to see the speaker clearly, it was Ed Henry.

Ed was at the gym a lot, too.. He pumped iron and often cut classes to do push ups. He was also a black belt Tae Kwan Do but was more comfortable with the gypsy crowd than the athletic fraternity. " The Red Dagger Society, as they call it, is pledged to restore "order", and return the campus to the days when men were men and giants strode the earth. Many of them are second, third, even fourth generation legacies. Until now, I would have thought they were just a bunch of blowhards, but I am not so sure. Everyone needs to be careful. These guys can react like a pack of wolves. I don't see any of them hunting alone."

A pall fell over the room. Woody said, "Phase I of Operation Jock Itch will be to create fear with certain girlfriends of guys we are pretty sure are in the Red Dagger. Henry has four names, two of whom are sisters, Allegra and Gabriella Donovan. Tonight we will place a few calls and nothing too hard or nasty, but we will just shake them up. Email blasts will also begin. Meanwhile, I still need everyone to keep your ear to the ground. See what you can find out about what happened to Bob last night."

After a few questions were fielded the group filed out of the room. They were quiet but excited. Finally, the gypsies would strike back. As one of the last to leave, Ed Henry said to Woody, "I am not sure that is such a good idea. Those girls haven't done anything that we know of."

"Collateral damage," Woody replied smugly. All he could think of was inflicting as much pain as possible.

CHAPTER 12

Special Agent Bradley had spent all afternoon interviewing students who resided in McDonald Hall. He had never been in such a building as the older dorms presented. The exterior was built of large sandstone slabs into which were cut narrow rectangular window openings with old style crank out windows. Inside there was a large entry with a similar stone fireplace at one end and hallways leading off in two directions. Opposite the fireplace a staircase led up to the second and third floors. There was no such convenience as an elevator. One door in the entrance area was marked "Matron" for the "dorm mother" charged with looking out for her boys or turning in the troublemakers. In a small side room off the hallway SA Bradley had been able to question several of the students in the dorm.

No one had seen anything out of the ordinary on the prior night or heard any sounds of struggling or a fight. The old stone dorms and high ceiling rooms muffled all noise. Mrs. Harmon, the dorm mother, kept her door shut after 7 pm in the winter and likewise neither heard nor saw anything. One common thread he heard from several students was that Anderson had a lot of friends, mostly gypsies and that he would be missed. There was some talk that Anderson's room was the go to spot for "the good stuff" as one student related. Bradley made detailed notes in his pad. Later, I learned that as darkness approached he called Deputy Baker and they agreed to meet up at my house on Alabama

Avenue to compare notes.

By the time I got home, Yogi and Bradley were waiting for me in Yogi's cruiser that was idling in front of my house with the lights off. I invited them in and let Rocket out for her evening run. There was still enough snow around for her to get good and wet before woofing to come back in. Yogi had the fire going when I poured us all a few fingers of Jack Black and we settled into the chairs in my compact living room. Each of them filled me in on what they had learned, or not learned during the day.

"This has been one helluva day," I said rubbing my eyes with my palms.

"It ain't over yet Jack," Yogi said catching me a little off guard.

"What else could possibly go wrong?" I asked hoping we had seen the worst of this tragedy.

"There's something else going on here. I don't like how that dorm room was torn up," said Bradley, "it doesn't match with someone just trying to break shit, more like someone was looking for something." The thought sent a shiver up my back.

Yogi continued, "I'm getting the same sense. Anderson's girlfriend gave me his laptop computer which I have in my bag. I haven't had much chance to examine it but I found some very disturbing emails on Anderson's computer referring to someone called the "Mexican". If it's the same guy, law enforcement has heard of him. Our information is that a Mexican drug runner has set up operations in Tennessee. The location gives access to seventy per cent of the US population within an eight hour drive. Plus, all of the warehouses in and around Nashville are a perfect cover.."

"What?" I asked. I wasn't sure I had heard him correctly.

"I suspect the room was torn up by someone looking for what the kids call "the good stuff" or maybe his computer." Bradley offered. "They just didn't have enough time to complete the search before we showed up. I have made contact with the drug task force in our office that is working closely with the U.S. Attorney's Office out of Nashville. We may know more tomorrow."

"Are you trying to tell me that Anderson is a dealer hooked up with a Mexican drug runner?" I asked.

"Jack, we have suspected the campus was a distribution center for a long time, we just didn't have good enough intel to do anything about it." Yogi said. "We don't have anything specific on Anderson. Unless we catch something going down, it's clear students aren't going to rat out each other. But, now, things are different. We have recovered Anderson's computer. That may provide us with some answers."

I could tell Bradley was twitching like a cat trying to decide if he was going to spring on a bird or not. Bradley started talking about undercover stings, wiretaps and surveillance, at which point I cut him off: "Hey, just cool it g-man. We are not going to turn this campus into a carnival. I can remember how bad it got at Knoxville when the entire starting backfield of the football team went around stealing tv sets from the dorms. We don't need that here."

"Okay, Okay," Bradley said reluctantly. He was looking to Yogi for support but wasn't finding any.

After a second, I asked, "What do we know about who carried out the abduction of Anderson?"

Yogi responded, "the symbol stenciled on the sign looks like a knife covered in blood. Several kids I talked to mentioned something called the Red Dagger Society, but did not know any other details."

"I got the same reports. The Red Dagger Society sounds like a group of neo-conservative athletes who formed a secret society to preserve the "old values" on campus. No one could or would give me any names," Said SA Bradley.

" I hope my student investigators have more for me tomorrow. I meet early with Mr. Anderson's parents tomorrow," I said yawning as I barely finished the sentence. The Jack was starting to work. We all sipped a little more in contemplation of just how things were getting complicated as the fire crackled and spit. Then SA Bradley dropped the next bombshell:

"Our office has also been contacted by Mr. Anderson's father. It seems he is the Assistant United States Attorney for the northern district of Kentucky."

I just looked at him speechless. Things just got worse.

CHAPTER 13

In an assistant coach's office in the back of the football training facilities, a group of about fifteen young men were gathered waiting for two more. Ben Ray, captain of the track team, and Winston Campbell, starting quarterback on the football team were the last to arrive. Only the desk lamp with its opaque green shade provided any illumination in the cramped room as it painted faces with streaks of light and shadow likes ghouls around a dim fire. There was a hush over the assembled men. Word had gone out that a meeting of the Red Dagger Society had been called. Attendance was mandatory.

Winston started, "Okay, guys. It is time to circle the wagons. Our boy, Anderson, is not doing well. Rumor is that he is in a coma from exposure. You guys didn't leave him out in the snow did you?"

A huge lineman, Darius Jones, said, "Of course not. We had him inside the Cabin most of the night tied to a post. Sure he was only in his boxers, but there was a fire going. After we painted him up with molasses we took turns tossing handfuls of corn flakes at him. You know they stick better that way. Finally, someone cut open a pillow and dumped the goose down all over his ass."

A couple of hoots and laughs erupted. "Keep it down, guys" Ben said. "Tell me about how Anderson was doing during all this." Ben had a no bullshit demeanor.

Darius Jones continued, "He was scared shitless. Everyone had on a hood. I think we told him we were going to start putting out cigars on him for each exam where he cheated. Cigars were being lit around the Cabin. I remember Pete cut the pillow open with a big Bowie and told him his guts and nuts were next. That when I thought he had shit himself."

Someone else chimed in, "He was squealing like that guy in the *Deliverance* movie. Sooey, Sooey." Ben held his palms out in a downward motion to quell the laughter.

"And this went on for how long?" Winston asked.

"Hell, Winston, all night like we planned. He thought we were nuts, but he broke down after a while and the pussy just wanted us to let him go." Darius added.

"You know, all I said was to scare him, not to hurt him in any way." Winston countered.

"Nobody laid a hand on the little shit. After a while he just couldn't take it any longer and he started screaming and blabbering." Darius said. "Did you guys see anybody punch him or anything?" Darius looked around the room to see several guys shaking their heads. "I didn't think so." Of course, no one planned on contradicting Darius either.

"Sooey" someone said and the laughter erupted again.

Winston asked, " Are you sure no one saw you?"

Darius responded, " Don't think so. With all the snow there wasn't any traffic out there that I saw."

Then Winston said, "You all listen to me. Eyes on me!" He paused briefly his eyes sweeping the room like the quarterback he was, leading the team into the threat posed by the opposing squad. Only when he was sure he commanded everyone's attention, he continued, " Everyone keeps his mouth shut. The first guy who breathes a word of this will hurt us all. Just keep quiet and your ears open. No talk about the Red Dagger Society, no emails, no telephone calls, no Facebook, no nothing. If we don't hang together we will all hang separately." The room was now silent except for Darius whose thunderous breath filled the room like the concussion of distant fireworks.

"What happens next?" Darius asked.

Winston said, "Ben and I have got to figure this out. If nobody talks, they can't tie anything back to any of us. Ben, you are on the Honor Council so stay tuned into what is going on there. That new Dean, Mathews is his name, came around the KZ house the other night. We don't need him going all *Columbo* on us.. I think all this will blow over. We've just got to stay cool. Any questions?"

Ben spoke up, "I don't think we hurt that guy but if someone can tie it back to us and he doesn't make it, we are all in a world of hurt. No more meetings and no more talk until we know more. He was still screaming when I parked him at the Student Union."

Winston nodded at Ben. The members of the Red Dagger Society slithered down the back stair well. Ben and Winston locked up and were the last to leave. "What's the next move?" Ben asked.

"I need to talk to Braxton. He will have some ideas." While Winston was confident in his ability to think quickly and process information, he also valued his cousin's perspective, so before things flew apart he thought it best to see what Braxton thought. It was too late to reach Braxton at Quantico but soon he would talk with his mentor.

CHAPTER 14

My meeting the next morning with Bob Anderson's parents had not gone well. His mother who said little seemed to be in shock, but her husband, Robert, Sr. said enough for both of them. After informing me of his status as Assistant United States Attorney for Kentucky he threatened me, the school, the Trustees, and anybody who had anything to do with the assault on his son. One minute he was grilling me like the federal prosecutor he was, and the next guaranteeing me the FBI, Homeland Security and the Department of Justice would soon be involved. What a pompous ass! My world seemed filled with such people at the moment. His ranting and raving could be heard throughout the offices as if it would change anything. He was correct those agencies would soon be involved, but not as he had expected. After he left I returned to my desk preparing to call the school's lawyers.

Emails from Clendon Crawford and Tom Savage began to arrive later in the morning.

From Clendon: *Planning on initial meeting of the Honor Council tomorrow afternoon if I can find a quorum. I have a couple of leads. More later.*

And then from Savage: *Wombat says he is onto something. Everyone is going underground but thinks retaliatory actions are in the works from the gypsy side.* Retaliate? Really? I wondered.

My reply to each: *Thanks. Keep me updated.*

Emily Sellars pushed open my door, "Got a sec?" she asked.

"Sure." Emily could push my buttons but there was an attraction between us. Soon I would have to get up the nerve to ask her out. I came around the desk to sit once again in the high backed chair facing her and that coal black hair framing an angular face with high cheekbones. She had the slightest dimple on her right cheek when she smiled. Unfortunately, she was not smiling now. Her liquid turquoise eyes held mine and she began to apologize,

"Jack, I am sorry about yesterday. When I saw that poor guy it just made me sick. I was fearful I might throw up so I went home."

"It was pretty disgusting. I can't imagine what anyone was thinking to do that and I hope Mr. Anderson recovers soon," I said.

Emily responded, "Yes, we all do, but I need to let you know I have a couple of very upset girls in McCready Hall. The Donovan sisters. You know the two gorgeous twins from Texas."

I had not been on campus long enough to learn every student's name, but all the male population on the mountain was aware of the Donovan sisters. Super models had nothing on these girls. I had heard one dated the Captain of the football team and the other the captain of the track team. The fact that you never saw one without the other doubled the heavenly vision. I was distracted for a second but

Emily brought me back to the present,

"Late last night Allegra began receiving strange calls on her cell phone. About the same time Gabriella was flooded with emails."

"We all get spammed," I said, not overly concerned.

Emily said, "No, these were not spam, but directed specifically at these girls. Very hateful, scary and creepy. The calls to Allegra knew about her schedule, where she parked her car, and even her boyfriend. The caller seemed weird and it really got to her. The emails were of a similar nature."

I asked, "How long did this go on?"

"For hours," Emily said, then continued," They called me early and were both crying."

"Has anything like this happened before?" I asked.

"Not that has been reported to me." At that moment Tammy buzzed into my phone and said that Emily had another distraught girl on the line.

Emily said to put the call into her office. She rose and looked at me over her shoulder saying "Here we go again." Was this the retaliation planned by the gypsies?

In the few minutes that passed before she returned, I read more emails from my men in the field.

From Savage: *Wombat says the gypsies are almost giggly. He thinks they plan to retaliate against Red Dagger. Thinks the Red Dagger is controlled by someone off campus.*

From Crawford: *Can't get a quorum just yet to schedule meeting. Several members say they have too much going on with exams coming up. I will get together a list of potential witnesses. More later.*

This time Emily shut the door firmly as she entered my office, knocking a couple of my paddling photographs off center. I rose to straighten the shot of me and Yogi at Quarter Mile Rapid on the Nolichucky as she updated me.

"So, now I have reports from four more coeds of the same type of calls and emails that were sent to the Donovan sisters. The same creepy messages were sent to each of these girls."

I asked, "Is there any connection between any of these girls?"

Emily responded, "They all date football players or other athletes."

"OK, so maybe this is the gypsy response?" I asked, it being the only logical explanation.

"That's my guess, too. You should know the Donovan sisters have called their father, Tony Donovan. They live in Cameron County, Texas where he is in the import-export business doing a lot of business with China. He has dispatched a couple of assistants to protect his girls. I think we will hear from them tomorrow." Emily said.

What were two assistants of Mr. Anthony Donovan doing on the way to our little school? I was getting more concerned we were losing what little control there was over the situation. Yogi, SA Bradley and I needed to talk. I asked Emily to let me know if there were any more calls to the girls.

I caught up with Yogi and Bradley later at Anderson's dorm room.

Yogi nodded and said, "Wasn't this your room back in the day?"

"Yeah," I replied, "Open it up, I have an idea about something."

As Bradley removed the yellow crime scene tape, Yogi unlocked the door and we entered to find the whole room tossed. I had not been in this room for more than a decade but something did not feel right. Something was out of place.

"This is how we left it Monday. Someone was looking for something that I don't think they found, " Yogi said.

SA Bradley added, "I don't think whoever snatched Anderson had anything to do with this. The guys who grabbed and decorated Anderson were motivated to humiliate and maybe scare him, but this looks more like a search party."

As I wandered around the room gathering old

thoughts of lying in this same standard dorm bed looking up at the ceiling, it struck me that the strangeness I sensed involved the ceiling. Instead of the sprayed popcorn look, someone had installed a drop down metal system into which were inserted prefab squares forming a lower artificial ceiling.

"Yogi," I said, "I don't think I have seen a ceiling quite like this anywhere else in any dorm on campus. We don't use drop down ceilings."

We were all three staring up at this point when Bradley hopped up onto the bed and said "I think I can just reach this one." With his Maglite in his right hand he pushed up the square enough to see it was hanging on something that prevented it from sliding out of the way.

"We need a ladder boys," Bradley said as Yogi went to find a janitor's closet. He soon returned, ladder in tow and said,

"Step back. Let's see what we've got here". Yogi positioned the ladder beneath the tile Bradley had tried to lift and climbed so that he had leverage. With both hands he pushed the tile up and out of the way as something heavy slid to the side. The frame of the ceiling shook and for a moment I thought it was all coming down. Yogi pulled his flashlight out of his belt and said "Well, well, would you look at this?" Bradley and I strained our necks to see up into the blackness of the opening.

Yogi tugged as a deep plastic tool box inched toward the opening. He eased it down to his chest and handed it gingerly down to Bradley who dropped it onto the bed.

Bradley stepped back and reaching into his pocket extracted a pair of purple latex gloves. "Don't want to contaminate the scene," he explained. He moved back to the box and checked the lid, sides and edges for any sign of something foreign or anything that looked out of place. Once again he spoke looking at the box, "I don't see any evidence of a trip wire or booby trap." Bradley was a little dramatic but I was focused on the toolbox as he prepared to open it. Yogi having climbed down from the ladder looked over at me and shrugged as if to say "it's just Bradley being Bradley."

"I'll be damned, " said Bradley as he popped open the latch on either side of the toolbox. A deep tray full of dark pills occupied the top of the container. It must have been three inches deep and I guessed there were thousands of pills in that tray. As I looked around Bradley's shoulder he lifted out the tray and I could see in the lower compartment four or five wrapped bricks of something plus a bag of what must have been marijuana. Bradley opened the baggie and sniffed. He nodded and said, "Pretty sure that's grass." The one gallon freezer bag bounced up and down in his hand.

"Un-friggin' believable," Yogi added.

As Bradley sucked on his teeth he ran his purple fingers through the pills like a fall collection of field peas and said "What a shitload." I realized

Mr. Anderson or his roommate had been busy with more than just regular college life.

Bradley said, "If this is what I think it is, the street value of this stuff is way up there. Those pills are probably speed. At a couple of bucks apiece just the top tray is worth several thousand dollars. Just having possession of this almost guarantees someone a long stay at one of Tennessee's finest correctional facilities."

Yogi took custody of the toolbox as he relocked the room replacing the crime scene tape. I followed as Yogi and Bradley climbed down the three flights of steps and briskly walked to the patrol car. Yogi secured the toolbox in the trunk and with the trunk still open handed the laptop computer Autumn had given him to me.

"You need to know it is on the evidence list report already, and that my Uncle is serious about everything being logged in," Yogi said. "He has already grilled me about it."

I agreed to look through it and return it to Yogi soon.

By now it was growing dark so I hustled back down University Avenue to Alabama and turned left down the hill to my house laptop in hand. I don't know what compelled me to pull out my cell phone and push in seven numbers. The phone rang and when Emily picked up I said, "Want to come over for a drink?"

"Sure" Emily answered without hesitation. Apparently our courtship had begun.

CHAPTER 15

When he saw the number flash on his cell phone it always unnerved him. Even though the last thing he wanted was to answer this call, he knew he had no choice in the matter having passed the point of no return long ago.

Ominously the voice said, "I understand we have a little problem, my friend."

"Our associate has left school and his product was confiscated."

"What caused this?" said the Mexican.

"A college prank that flew out of control, I suspect" the First man said.

"But you will restore the control, no?" said the Mexican in a way that was more declarative than inquisitive.

"I am working on it now. There is a lot involved and several loose ends," the First man said.

"I am not a man who enjoys loose ends," said the Mexican in a measured deliberate voice. "My business operates with the smoothness of a senorita's cheek because everyone does his part. My friend, if you cannot do yours, I am afraid there will be consequences."

The First man knew there would be consequences. No one let the Mexican down without suffering such consequences. Consequences that only a man lacking all compassion or forgiveness like the Mexican could deliver. There had been others before the First man who had failed the Mexican only to be visited by his agents after which they had never been seen again at least not in these parts.

Contemplating this, the First man said, "I am restoring control and order. Even now I am replacing our associate."

The Mexican said, "Good. You should locate our associate's computer and his inventory and secure both."

"I am afraid there is a little problem with that," said the First man.

That was not information a man such as the Mexican was prepared to hear. There was silence on the line for a few seconds, then the Mexican spoke,

"Three of my men are on the way to you. They will assist you in the recovery of the product and the computer. Their leader is a man named Elias."

First man said, "Mr. Elias is already here. We have spoken and he is prepared to recover the computer tomorrow."

"Good," the Mexican said, "then call me back tomorrow with better news." The line went dead.

CHAPTER 16

The blocky Lincoln Continental pulled into the gravel lot at the Mountain Truck Stop just off Interstate 24 at the peak of the over mountain pass as midnight approached. Two large men in dark suits and dark ties sporting fedoras and sunglasses climbed out of the car the gravel crunching under their heavy shoes. Even at such an hour there were a few drivers in the café eating pastry and sipping thick black coffee from white stained mugs while swapping road stories. A George Jones ballad played in the background and the occasional sound of dishes being stacked escaped from the kitchen through the swinging door. From time to time hookers, or road "lizards" as the truckers called them, would set up in such a place. Occasionally, a student cramming for exams and in need of a pecan waffle smothered in syrup would wander in. But not tonight. Tonight only a handful of truckers spoke in low tones as the two strangers strode into the café.

Drago drug a metal chair across the concrete floor and sat where he had a clear sight line to the glass front door and the kitchen. Habit and caution had taught him to claim the high ground and to always, always be prepared. However, Drago was no Boy Scout. His broad Sicilian forehead was overrun with a diagonal scar that just missed his left eye. With fingers the size of sausages he wrapped a paw cleanly around one of the mugs Angelo sat down on the table. This late you picked up what you wanted from the counter and served yourself unless you needed to order in which case a stocky surly woman in a white apron with a cigarette dangling from one side of her mouth would ask "What you want, sugar?". Regulars had learned that when she said "How do you like your eggs?" she would immediately slap you if you wise cracked "I just love them little sunsofbitches." This waitress had no sense of humor. She had been on her feet dealing with truckers, hookers and punk students for too many years.

Angelo was negligibly smaller than his brother and barely two years younger. Each of the men had worked for the padrone or his family their entire adult lives solving problems or quelling nuisances like the fools who were harassing the daughters of a very powerful businessman like Antonio Donovan.

As the strangers settled in Angelo patted the snug fitting H&K .40 caliber pistol under his arm just to be sure it was there. Drago admonished him not to be so obvious since they already looked out of place amongst the half dozen truck drivers in blue jeans and Carharts. It wasn't as if either of them needed to carry weaponry. Angelo could kill a man ten ways with his bare hands and if Drago got close enough he could crush a man's throat like snapping a twig. It was the secure feeling Angelo had knowing he had the loaded pistol so close with a suppressor and extra clip in his pocket. They had been in tight situations before and it was always prudent not to carry a knife to a gun fight. Who knew what this assignment would involve?

A crumpled copy of the student newspaper, *The Purple Onion*, lay on the table open to the lead story about something called The Red Dagger Society, a group called "gypsies", and the investigation being conducted by local police and the university obviously left by a student who had taken a break from studying to grab one of the famous waffles. This was fortunate thought Drago as he scanned the article for any information he could use in search of the fool or fools who were bothering Allegra and Gabriella. He noted the byline "by Jim Wombat" on the article. He intended to move quickly and decisively and perhaps this Mr. Wombat would be his first point of contact. From Allegra he knew the Red Dagger boys were the good guys. With his smartphone Drago quickly connected to the University website and pulled up a photograph and email address for Mr. Wombat. No one knew at the time this would be the last time the school server or website would work for several days. Drago's plan was to lure Wombat into meeting him and Angelo to "share" information about the harassment. Once he identified the target, Drago would move without delay and resolve the issue. Muscle like Drago and Angelo would advance like an irresistible force leaving all opposition crushed and smoldering before they could react.

Wombat typically rose early since his head was clearer and he wrote more creatively at that point in the day. He had received a cryptic email inviting him to meet with a gentleman from out of town who had information regarding the Red Dagger Society. Wombat, imagining himself like Bernstein or

Woodward could not pass up this clandestine rendezvous with his own version of "Deepthroat" so he stuffed his pad into an overcoat and headed off to the Student Union. Crossing the street near the edge of the Quad, Wombat saw that most of the snow had melted except where it lay piled in mounds having been scraped by the county trucks to open at least one traffic lane after the weekend's storm. By the curb a large dark car idled. The window rolled down and a heavily accented voice said, "Mr. Wombat please join us."

When Wombat was on the trail of a good story, little got in his way, especially his common sense or any apprehension of danger. Wombat was short, pudgy and believed like the Rumpole character that "physical exercise was a short cut to the cemetery." Without any hesitation he climbed into the rear of the Lincoln and as it pulled away he heard the faintest hint of a soft click from the door.

A large man turned in his seat to address him, "Mr. Wombat, thank you for agreeing to meet with us. It is our hope you can provide us with some information about the current situation that is developing at this school. I have read your article in the newspaper and I have questions about this "gypsies"".

"What possible interest could you have regarding anything at this school?" asked Wombat now wondering what he was doing in this large dark car and where he was going.

"Let's say it is personal. It is about family," said the man slowly. The other man who was driving occasionally glanced at Wombat in the rear view mirror. He nodded and repeated the word "Family." Wombat had hardly noticed they had driven past the campus and were headed to a secondary gravel road that would ultimately wind its way down the backside of the mountain.

All the moisture in Wombat's throat had vaporized. When Wombat did not respond right away, the man continued, "You see Mr. Wombat, our employer has daughters at this school who have been harassed by these gypsies. We intend the harassment should stop yesterday."

Sensing it was his turn to speak, Wombat offered, "All I can tell you is that the gypsies are a group of non-conformist students. They do not belong to any fraternities or sororities, nor do they belong to any organized athletic teams. Some of them are very bright but they generally stick to themselves and avoid other student functions."

The large man said, "We think you know much more than this, Mr. Wombat. I am sure you want to help us don't you?"

Wombat could feel the sweat beginning to trickle down his back as he slyly reached for the door handle only to confirm that the click he heard earlier was the sound of his imprisonment.

"Mr. Wombat, our friends are rewarded but those who are unhelpful become our enemies. Our enemies do not fare well. Why is it you wish to become our enemy?" asked the man whose features were just becoming visible in the pre-dawn light.

Now, Wombat's alarms were sounding loudly. His reporter instinct told him not to talk since it was his role to gather information by listening rather than speaking. Never give up a source, or a friend, and he was a friend to Henry Chen, his roommate, his source for all information regarding the gypsies. Yet, the present circumstances were unlike any situation he had experienced. Swiftly the large man's hand cleared the front seat and pinned Wombat to the seat like a bug.

"It is time Mr. Wombat, for you to answer our questions. Who are the gypsies. Give us names. We will start with their leader," insisted Drago pushing a little harder with his hand into the softness of Wombat's chest.

"He...he...he...," stumbled Wombat, "is in the hospital." Wombat's eyes had grown wide and it was hard to breathe. Suddenly, he had the urge to pee but begged his bladder "don't, please don't."

"Yes, we read. Poor Mr. Anderson. In his absence, who are the most visible of this group?"

Wombat's mind was now scrambling for names as the iron fist kept its pressure on his chest. He felt like that cartoon of a mouse giving the finger to the eagle as he was held in its talon. Desperate as he was, even Wombat was not so stupid as to give the finger to this guy. Names rushed through his head of likely gypsies, but all he could think of was Henry and then of course! Woody German. Good old Woody, what a piss ant thought Wombat. He blurted out "Woody German, he's the guy. He is in the same dorm as Anderson. McDonald Hall. He has dark hair and, and....a pony tail" There, he had given them an answer and cleverly omitted naming Henry Chen. Or so, he thought.

"Mr. Wombat we plan to visit Mr. German shortly. If he is not what you say, we will return to visit with you and next time we will not be so....hospitable. Now get out." Drago demanded.

"But, we are miles away from campus," squeaked Wombat.

All he heard was laughing as the Lincoln pulled away. Wombat was stranded halfway down the mountain on a muddy gravel road. He was going to be late for class. So much for Bob Woodward.

CHAPTER 17

The early morning sun had begun to paint the tops of the evergreens as I ran along the old fence row by the field that once stabled the university's horses. When Rocket and I had left the house that morning I debated whether or not to wear sweats, but decided to ignore the chill and run in shorts and a hoodie. Once the blood was circulating my legs would not even notice that it was still cold outside. My breath was barely visible in front of me as I let my gaze drift across the fields and down the gravel road bordered by the wire fencing held up by chestnut posts. No one took care of this fence row any longer and the horse population had been sold off years ago. A lone coyote stopped on a raised knob and turned as I passed judging whether I was threat or food. I had hit one of those plateaus on this run where I was on cruise control breathing easily legs striding effortlessly. In this state I felt I could run all day. This is what distance running was all about. Piss on the sprinters, and the hurdlers too. Whatever chemicals this run was producing in my brain carried me to a different calm place.

Rocket kept up with me although with her darting around to survey interesting smells she probably ran twice what I did. I knew I had to be careful that she did not overdo the run. Once, when she was around six months old we had run so far the next day she couldn't even walk until the soreness worked itself out. We got back to my house in time for a shower, a bagel and a cup of coffee I would pick up from the Brew Shop on the way to the office.

"Boss, we have a problem," Tammy announced as I stepped into the foyer. "Look". She swiveled her computer screen around for me to see. All I could see was the shriveled face of an old old woman. The screen was a black and white photograph perhaps from an old movie still.

"What are you looking at?" I asked.

"You don't understand. She is looking at me and it's on all the computers, " Tammy reported.

I stepped into my office to find that Tammy had fired up my computer earlier and just as I had seen on her screen the penetrating eyes of a very old foreign looking woman with a flat nose stared back at me. Below her face appeared the words:

EVEN A MAN WHO IS PURE IN HEART

AND SAYS HIS PRAYERS AT NIGHT

MAY BECOME A WOLF WHEN THE WOLF'S BANE BLOOMS

AND THE AUTUMN MOON IS BRIGHT.

"What in the hell?" I said as the lovely Ms. Sellars stepped out of her office and into mine.

Approaching my desk she said, "I've got the same thing and I can't make it go away."

My cell phone started ringing and all over

campus reports were coming in from faculty and students that every computer was displaying the same image. Our system was locked up and apparently someone had taken control over the primary computer server for the University. Land lines that ran through the server were likewise inoperable. The school was effectively shut down and back to the Dark Ages. No one could use email or access any records. The Registrar's Office could not process any monetary transactions coming in or going out, so they gave up, locked the door and went home. Lacking the ability to pull up outlines and course materials which were stored on the University server according to policy, most faculty cancelled classes. The President sent a hand written note to me that this was unacceptable. I jotted him a reply that I was not the IT person but we were working on the problem.

Something about the old woman who stared at me was familiar. Her gray hair pulled back and covered with a scarf exposed large ring-shaped earrings. Those eyes burned into my head stirring an old memory. I had seen her before but where and what in the hell did the message mean?

"Mrs. Allgood please get the University's information technology officer and the professor who runs the computer sciences lab in my office as quickly as possible," I instructed. The old woman continued to stare at me as I doodled the word "gypsy" on my legal pad. I was still contemplating what this meant when the IT officer, Pete Norman, and professor Ken Jones were led in by Tammy

Allgood.

"Gentlemen, please have a seat, " I said as we gathered around my circular table. "We seem to have an issue with the computer system. What can you tell me."

Norman began, "Sometime last night a virus infected and assumed control over our server with the result that any connection to the server was likewise corrupted."

"So when will you have it fixed?" I asked.

"Who knows, Jack. This is a very sophisticated "hack" into our system by a very skilled operator. So far I have isolated the attack as originating from Europe, perhaps Romania," answered Norman. He continued, "It could be days before we crack the password letting us into the virus program. Once inside we should be able to turn it off."

"Days?" I asked my tension growing by the minute. "We do not have days. This school is shut down. I need answers now. I cannot imagine why this school's computer system would attract Eastern European hackers. Something doesn't feel right about this, something sophomoric like a college prank." An idea was sparking in my head, " I want you to include in your considerations the possibility that this virus originated right here on campus."

Norman and Jones looked at each other before Norman asked, "What makes you think this could have originated here?"

I explained, "For the past few days we have been dealing with a situation where a student was assaulted and left in front of the Student Union. This victim is part of a subgroup on campus that call themselves the "Gypsies". I don't think this woman is a coincidence. " I pointed at the image and said, "She's a gypsy woman. I am concerned that the attack on our computer system is some kind of retaliatory response by the Gypsy group against the University and the group who captured and tortured the victim."

Now, I had their attention so I went on, "The picture on the screen of the old woman is the same on every computer screen on campus, is it not?" The both nodded. I could tell they had not even considered our attack could be home grown.

The eyes of the old woman continued to haunt us as I continued my theory, "I think the identifying message below the image tells us what we need to know. Either of you guys remember the old 1930s movie *The Wolfman*? I think this actress played an old gypsy and recited those lines to Lon Chaney Jr. after he was bitten by the original man wolf, her son. I think this movie is the key we need." I recalled watching that movie many times late on Saturday night as a kid and having to cover my eyes when the transformation began from man into wolf.

Norman said, "That is an interesting theory. I can use facts from that movie to see if I can trigger a password. However, since we have lost all internet connection I will have to do the research from the library. It won't be quick but I will get to it. Are we sure that anyone on this campus has the skills to pull this off. " He look inquisitively at the professor.

"I have one student with exceptional insight into computers. He worked with the University to set up all email accounts when we went to the Spectrum Server last year. If he was able to take control over the Administrator function of our email he could have gotten into our system, " said the professor, "but, I cannot imagine that he would do something like this."

"Who is this student, " I asked.

"His name is Henry Chen, " offered the professor.

I asked Tammy to bring me Mr. Chen's file. Opening the folder I noted his dorm and roommate. The name "James Wombat" was typed in. "Tammy, please have someone go ask Mr. Wombat to come here." I asked the professor to contact Mr. Chen. The professor and Mr. Norman left on their assignments while I thought about my theory and how to check it out.

CHAPTER 18

Woody German didn't even see it coming as he started to open the door to his dorm room. One second he was reaching for the knob, then something hit him in the back of the head and he blacked out. Sometime later when consciousness slowly crawled back into his brain he realized he was tied in his wooden desk chair, his mouth was gagged, and he either couldn't see or was blind folded or the lights were off. Woody flexed both hands but couldn't move anything but his fingers. A voice broke the silence:

"Looks like sleeping beauty has decided to wake up," said a voice from the darkness.

A different voice said, "How's the head, college boy?"

Woody then remembered being hit and now his head hurt like a sonofabitch. He struggled to say something but with his mouth taped it came out as a muffled grunt.

"Tell you what. I've got a deal for you. We're going to take the tape off your mouth if you promise to be a good boy, and not shout or anything. Capiche? But if you act up, you will be sorry and it's going to hurt. Nod if you agree," said the first man huskily.

Woody nodded which made his head hurt worse. Hands ripped the duct tape off his mouth yanking hair and skin along with it. He gasped, his heart racing, his head pounding and now his face on fire.

The first man then said, "Mr. German, you belong to a group known as the "gypsies"?"

Woody nodded still tightly bound at his arms, wrists and feet in the straight backed chair.

"Good. Correct answer, don't you think Angelo?" said the first man.

"He is a smart one, Drago. He understands how this is played." Said the second voice.

Woody squirmed testing his bindings but a quick slap across his face made him see bright lights. Now he was really hurting.

"Be still, college boy. Angelo really wants to play with you, and who knows before we're through I may let him have a little fun. We want you to understand that you and your friends have made a very bad mistake, " said Drago.

Woody managed to squeak out "We haven't,... I haven't done anything."

Before he finished the utterance the unseen hand sprung out once again and caught him across the nose this time. More lights, more pain, and now blood was running down his chin.

"Mr. German, you know the Donovan sisters? Two lovely girls, who happen to be the daughters of our employer. It seems that you or some of your friends in this "gypsy" group have been harassing these girls. And that, causes great stress to the padrone, " said Drago. A moment passed and no one said anything. Woody's breathing was coming short and fast.

Drago continued, "What stresses our employer, naturally stresses us. When we become stressed we are likely to do crazy things to relieve this stress. You and your friends have become a nuisance. Much like a mosquito that needs to be swatted. You understand?"

Woody, terrified, nodded. The two men grunted. It seemed this college boy was getting the message.

Drago spoke, "Now, your little fun is over. It is over for good. We want you to take a message back to your friends. The message is simple. Leave the Donovan girls alone. If any of you bothers them again, Angelo and I will return. If we return we will not be happy. If we are not happy the first person we will visit will be you, Mr. German. You do not want to see what we do when we are unhappy. Then, when we are done with you, we will visit each and every person who thinks they are a "gypsy". Do you understand what I am telling you?"

Woody nodded. He didn't think he could speak with the blood bubbling around his lips. He just wanted them to leave. His whole head hurt and he expected his nose was broken. Breathing from his mouth was forming blood bubbles on his lips but breathing through his nose was now impossible.

"So that we are certain you get the message, we will remain close for the next few days. Angelo make sure Mr. German knows we are men of our word," said Drago.

Angelo stepped to Woody and grabbed his left hand. A knife appeared in his hand and he sliced through the duct tape binding Woody's left arm and hand. Woody relaxed slightly as his left arm and hand came free. He felt the icy touch of the unseen man on his arm. Angelo admired the hand as Woody looked on helplessly. Then Angelo grabbed the pinkie finger and jerked it back until it snapped. When the top of the pinkie touched the top of his hand Woody screamed. Angleo then grabbed the next finger and repeated the transaction. Woody's screams filled the room but he was no longer conscious when Angelo got to the middle finger.

As silently as they had come into the room they left. It was dark outside and the dimly lit hallway was empty. This had been an easy assignment for the two Sicilians. The Lincoln pulled away from the street and down toward an old enclosed development used as summer cottages to escape the heat of the lowlands. Mr. Donovan had provided his cottage for their stay. While they expected no more issues from the gypsies, it was best to verify the message had been received loud and clear. So, they would roost on the mountain for a few days before returning to the wild hills of Texas.

CHAPTER 19

Yogi and Rockie stopped by my office and reported that the drugs we had found in Bob Anderson's room had been taken to the TBI lab in Nashville. Their interviews of students in McDonald dorm had not developed much if any new information on Anderson's abduction or anything new regarding the Red Dagger Society.

Yogi said, "Jack have you had a chance to look at the Anderson lap top computer yet? I am going to need to turn that into our evidence room soon. My uncle is asking that everything be bagged and tagged. He knows about the laptop. He just wants an inventory be completed. I am going to have to secure all the evidence, complete my report and I can't be leaving anything out."

Anderson's computer was sitting on my desk. I knew Yogi would not be able to stall for much longer in completing his report to the Sheriff. I replied to Yogi," Not yet. Give me another day or so. It has been crazy around here. Our entire university network has been shut down for a few days." I pointed at my monitor where the old lady glared. Yogi looked back at the old woman and once again surprised me with the ocean of information sloshing around in his head.

"Maria Ouspenskaya," Yogi said spontaneously.

"Who?" Bradley asked.

Yogi answered, "She's the old gypsy from the original Wolfman movie. I think she was a Russian actress. In the movie she only appears at night in the fog on the moors. Her son was also a wolfman and he bit the Lon Chaney, Jr. character before he beat him to death with his silver wolf headed cane." Yogi's head was stacked with row after row of useless trivia. He knew all that old movie shit. I had made the movie connection, but to come up with the actual name of a dead Russian actress? Impressive.

I said, "We think it may be part of a retaliatory strike by the gypsy group here on campus in response to the Anderson thing."

Yogi thought a minute. "Pretty clever. You remember how you kill the wolfman, Jack?" asked Yogi.

"Sure. A silver bullet," I said with emphasis. After contemplating this for another few seconds, I said, "We are looking for passwords to break into the virus and "silver bullet" could be the clue we have been missing." Bradley was lost. He wasn't familiar with the movie and couldn't keep up while Yogi and I almost finished each other's sentences. I told them I would pass along this information to the crew who were trying to defeat the virus.

Yogi and Bradley left saying they were going to make one more pass through Anderson's room and then head back to the station. They nodded at Tom Savage and Clendon Crawford who had arrived for the afternoon meeting to brief me.

Crawford said, "I have the first meeting of the Honor Council set for next Monday. It has not been easy getting everyone to commit since we are so close to finals, but I let them all know this was important. I plan to issue requests that certain students appear as witnesses. We cannot force anyone to come but I am hoping we get some cooperation."

I asked, "Good. Who is on your list of witnesses?"

Crawford said, " President of the Kappa Zetas, President of the Sigma Deltas, since most of their members are football and basketball players, then various other students who we have heard may know something. We are not looking into specific allegations regarding Mr. Anderson since he is still in the hospital, but I thought we would start with The Red Dagger Society and see where it went."

I noticed Savage had pulled out a pad and was jotting notes furiously.

"Don't you print a God-damn word of this," I warned waiving my finger at him.

Savage looked up and smiled. "It's for the historical record of these events," he quipped.

Not convinced of his motive, I said, "What have you found out?"

Savage said, " What I have learned is that The

Red Dagger Society is a secret campus group whose members are generally athletes. Membership is very select and it is actually quite old, older than several fraternities. Think "Skull and Bones" or the other secret societies at Harvard or Yale. For the most part it has been a quiet social group, but in the past year or so it has become more active. No one admits being a member, and no one can identify a member or when they meet, or where, or why. The fact that it has existed on campus for at least one hundred years but has remained so secretive is very unusual. It may have been dormant for years only to awaken when something is triggered. I don't have a clue why it exists or what could be the trigger. I'm still digging but my ace, Jim Wombat, was on a good lead but now he has been missing for more than a day. It's not like him to miss classes and not check in with the *Purple* staff. I am getting a little worried about him."

"He'll show up. When I was a student here I never heard of The Red Dagger Society," I said. "To my knowledge, before this Anderson thing, they had never caused any trouble or harmed anyone."

"Still, they have claimed credit for the Anderson feathering, and that tells us something, I'm just not sure what," said Savage.

I asked Crawford if he thought I should attend the Honor Council meeting next week. He asked if he could think about it, and they left. I was convinced I should be there as a symbol of the seriousness with which we took this investigation.

Before leaving my office I considered putting Anderson's laptop into the safe that sat next to Tammy's desk. The safe was deceptively designed to resemble a table on which she had put a lamp and a picture of her and Leon next to a red pickup truck. Only Tammy, Emily and I knew it was in reality a strong box. Instead, I copied Anderson's hard drive files onto a thumb drive, locked the thumb drive in the safe, put the laptop into my briefcase, turned out the lights, locked up and headed for home. I knew Rocket would be anxious to get out. I had no clue how important that laptop would become, or that three suspicious men were looking for it and for me.

CHAPTER 20

Wombat had never been so cold and tired in his life. Step by step he pulled his pudgy little body up the muddy mountain road climbing in sweeping curves as it cutback across the backside of the campus. With every step he was mumbling to himself "stupid, stupid." He had been at this climb all day and had only covered a couple of miles. Not a single vehicle had passed going either direction. When it got dark and he couldn't see to walk any further he attempted to climb up the bank on the right side. It took all his strength to crawl hand over hand as he pushed himself up with his toes a few inches only to slide back almost as far as he had progressed. He smelled of wet composted leaves and mud, but he was fortunate a front had passed through leaving night temperatures near forty degrees. He tried not to think of how chilled and hungry he was and what those two goons had been up to. Wombat was a city boy, not an outdoorsman. He hadn't even made it through his Tenderfoot badge in the Boy Scouts. One camping trip in the rain was enough to convince him that the hard ground was not meant to sleep on. Finally, he had made it far enough to grab hold of a tree trunk enabling him to pull himself the last few feet to a flat spot where he sat with his back to the road looking into the dark woods.

Wombat had a sense that things were crawling on him. His round spectacles were smeared and wet with mud. He imagined forest insects and bugs in his ears, his nose, his eyes.

Cackling barred owls called to each other as if to alert the entire forest a stranger was present and to be on guard. In his head the old rhyme "the worms crawl in, the worms crawl out, ..." played over and over about to drive him crazy. He had never heard the wild scream of barred owls and the sound added to the terror he sensed. Instead of the "who cooks for you" distinctive call, these owls accented different syllables and often did not complete the verse as they screamed at him. He was in a haunted wood and was sure he would die, his body consumed by flesh eating rodents.

Sometime during the night he must have fallen asleep because he awoke shaking violently as the first light came stabbing through the tops of the trees. Wombat knew enough about hypothermia to realize his body was in trouble and that he needed to get moving.

Wombat stood up and after taking a good long pee, he slid back down the embankment landing in the ditch with a splash to continue his trudge up the road. Although he had survived the night, his terror and pain were not resolved. His shoes were wet and sloshed with every step. He could feel his feet shriveling into tender wrinkled little fleshy things resembling uncooked chicken. More and more light filtered through the forest giving him a perspective that suggested he was still miles from the top. He began to cough and knew he would perish out in this forsaken place.

He was also starving, his stomach cramping for

lack of food. It was not that he lacked a fat layer that should last him awhile, but he was really hungry. Beneath a thin tree he noticed some kind of round fruit on the ground with which he was not familiar. Beyond ripe he picked up one of the objects and sniffed at the earth sweetness of the thing. The aroma wasn't offensive so he licked the outside of the pulpy vessel. That didn't kill him either so he took a bite and swallowed. Not bad, he thought so he ate the whole thing and six more after that. He didn't even wonder why squirrels or chipmunks had not cleaned up all these delicacies in the late fall when they matured. Only later in the throes of diarrhea would he question the wisdom of eating an unknown object off the forest floor.

He could not have been shuffling for more than a few minutes when below he could hear the murmur of an engine. Stopping to look down he saw a pickup truck's headlights navigating the switchbacks below him bouncing from right to left. At least it's not a Lincoln thought Wombat. Within a few minutes the truck pulled along side and the driver lowered the window.

"What in the world are you doing out here," asked Leon Allgood.

"It's a long story," said Wombat, "Can I catch a ride back to school?"

"Hop in Buddy. You are a mess," said Leon. The inside of Leon's truck was the finest vehicle Wombat had ever seen. It was warm and Mr.

Allgood had a dozen Krispy Kreme donuts he had picked up for the guys at work. "Go ahead. You look like you could use some energy," Leon said.

Wombat swallowed four donuts whole and told Leon what he had been through over the past day.

"Two big thugs in a Lincoln, huh. Can't say I've seen them around, but I'll keep a lookout," Leon said.

Wombat thanked him profusely as Leon dropped him at his dorm. It was still early, and in their dorm room Henry was asleep. Jim Wombat fell out of his wet khakis into a warm shower and then put on fresh clothes. Still moving slowly and quietly so as not to disturb Henry, Wombat sat at his desk and punched the "on" button for his laptop. Immediately, he was looking into the same face as everyone else on campus. Nothing he did would let him escape the image of the old gypsy. Trancelike, Wombat eyes fixed on the woman's eyes. He couldn't say how long he remained in that state, but he heard Henry stir from the top bunk and drop to the floor with a thud.

"Where in the fuck have you been?" Henry asked rubbing the sleep from his eyes.

"Henry, someone is looking for you. Big ugly guys in a black Lincoln. They grabbed me and dumped me down the old road leading down to the valley. They were asking about the gypsies and wanted names. Your name is all I could think of," Wombat stuttered.

"Shit! You gave them my name?" Henry asked excitedly.

"No," mumbled Wombat, now almost asleep, "I gave them Woody German." Pointing at his computer screen, Wombat asked, "Did you have anything to do with this?"

Henry hurriedly put on his clothes and said, "You don't need to know, Jim. Best to stay out of it. I may be out of pocket for a couple of days." Henry grabbed his backpack and was gone. Wombat crashed into the lower bunk asleep before he hit the mattress.

CHAPTER 21

Rocket was not waiting for me when I opened the door which should have been my first clue something was wrong. As I apprehensively stepped into my house I could smell the odor of cooked spicy meat. I hadn't cooked anything like that recently, and I was sure the garbage had been taken out. Sampson was not there either to greet me with his "mrrow, mrrow" welcome. Surely, they must both be racked out somewhere. My keys jingled as I dropped them into the bowl and turning I saw three Hispanic looking men in my living room. One stood by the window, another by the bookcase, and a third man sat in my favorite chair. I could see pistols dangling from the hands of two of the men. My jaw clenched and my lips were tight across my teeth.

"Can I help you?" I asked as I sat down my briefcase. My pulse had picked up and I did not know if my body was signaling fight or flight. The seated man was not holding a gun but a glistening large switchblade knife with a pearl handle. He motioned for me to sit, and I did. Taco wrappers were strewn on my coffee table which further indicated Rocket had not been in this room, else she would have been in the middle of that food. The men continued to stare.

"What do you want? And, where is my dog?" I asked now starting to grow angry. My fists flexed and unflexed as I unconsciously prepared to do something, but what my course of action would be was not readily apparent. I could feel my shoulders tense and kept my feet apart in case I had to move suddenly.

"Your dog is safe, and so long as you cooperate, she will remain that way. My name is Elias," said the man from the lounge chair. My mind kept racing among alternatives. I could jump up and run out the door, or I could jump up and run toward my bedroom closet where I had a Benelli semi-automatic 12 gauge shotgun, or I could run for the kitchen and a butcher knife, or I could sit there and listen. None of my options presented any likelihood of success. For the moment the only thing that made sense was to find out what they wanted and maybe they would leave.

"Who are you guys?" I asked.

"That's not important. All you need to know is that we are associates of a man who wants something you have taken, senor," said the man in a thick Latino accent.

"If I can help you I will, but I don't have a clue what you are after," I answered. My mouth was as dry as a cracker fart, as Yogi liked to say.

The man scratched his chin with the back of the knife blade before he spoke again. The man leaning against the bookcase shifted his weight to his other leg and the man at the window was staring out into the evening darkness. The seated man continued, "We believe you have a computer that belongs to a Mr. Anderson, is that not correct?"

How would these guys know that? No one but Yogi knew I had the laptop. "I still don't know what you are talking about," I said hoping to stall and drag more information out of them. It didn't work. The man at the window pointed his gun at me and then at the floor as he pulled the trigger launching one slug into my hardwood floor. I jumped as the firing pin made contact with the cartridge replacing the meaty smell with that of cordite. Splinters flew all over the floor, some striking my pants leg.

"Shit!" I exclaimed. I was trying to stay cool, and not mess my pants.

"Wrong answer, senor," said the first man who now waived the blade in my direction. "You are wasting our time." The less time I spent with these men, the better. Out of options I decided to give up the laptop knowing a copy of the hard drive remained in the office safe.

"Okay, okay," I said holding my palms out. "Look in my briefcase over there by the table."

Seated man nodded at window man who walked over and picked up my brief case, an LL Bean canvas bag with a large central pocket into which I had slipped Anderson's laptop. Window man pulled the computer out and let the briefcase fall to the floor. After handing the computer to seated man he resumed his station at the window.

The man called Elias smiled and said "Thank you."

A few minutes later seated man had turned on Anderson's computer and confirmed it was in fact what he was looking for.

"If you are a smart man you will forget you ever saw us. Do not call the police and do not try to follow us. If we find out differently we will be back to visit with you again," said the first man who was now rising. Closing the switchblade with one hand he continued to use the knife for emphasis tapping the closed handle against his other palm.

"Your dog is in the bedroom. She is sleeping off a little something we gave her. If we have to come back the dog will leave with us," threatened the man. He looked over at Standing Man and asked, "How long do you think such a pretty dog will last in the pit, Hector?" Standing Man and Window Man both snickered their teeth showing yellow beneath greasy moustaches.

I licked my lips considering whether I should say something macho or taunt these guys. Fortunately, my common sense had not completely left me and although what I wanted to do was to strike the man in the throat, I nodded. The man with the blade walked around my living room as if to assess my belongings. Then he turned and all three ambled out the front door. They did not hurry making a statement that they owned me. I glanced out the window to confirm they had left and I swear it looked like they had gotten into a police car of some kind. At least the car had police lights on top but I couldn't make any positive identification.

Scrambling back to the bedroom I flung the door open seeing Rocket lifeless in the bed, her mouth taped shut. I placed my hands on her chest and I could barely sense a rise and fall of her chest in a shallow rhythm. I kissed her head and slowly removed the tape careful not to pull too much hair with it. "Oh my sweet, sweet girl," I said over and over. Rocket stirred slightly but remained in a deep sleep. I didn't see any blood or signs of other physical injury. Meanwhile, Sampson's head pushed back the sheet from under the bed and he said "mrrow, mrrow". I gave him a neck scratch around his collar and told him it was going to be ok.

All I could think was if those guys had hurt Rocket I would have hunted them down and killed them. Big talk. Me and my 12 gauge. I needed to talk with Yogi so I dialed up his cell phone.

"Yo," said Yogi.

Shakily and a bit emotional I said, "I was just paid a visit by three grease balls who were looking for Anderson's computer."

"Anderson's computer? You didn't give it to them did you?" asked Yogi.

"Sorry but I did, Yogi, one of them blew a hole in my floor and they had done something with Rocket. She's ok I think, but I didn't have much choice. What I don't understand is how they knew it was with me," I explained.

Yogi didn't respond, but in that pause the

frightening realization came that Yogi was the only one who knew I had the laptop. Now, my mind screamed could I trust even Yogi?

CHAPTER 22

When the call with Jack disconnected, Yogi headed straight for the Sequoyah County Jail which also served as the Sheriff's offices. He pulled up and parked out front noticing that his was the only patrol car in the lot. Up a small flight of brick steps he entered the jail and nodded at the receptionist. He walked around her station and went through the door marked "Authorized Personnel Only." This led down a hallway with offices on each side and the evidence room at the end.

"Where is everybody, Pete?" Yogi asked leaning across the counter to the short man who sat behind the metal desk.

Pete looked up and nonchalantly said, "Jerry and Jonah went to answer a report of a wreck out on 31. Larry and Jug Ears went to grab something to eat."

"Where's Buford?" Yogi asked.

"He got a telephone call and left in a hurry. I think he's checked out for the day," Pete said.

"Hey, has anyone been looking at the File on that student who got decorated with molasses and feathers the other day?" Yogi asked.

"I haven't seen it. Buford has taken a special interest in that one. I think it's on his desk," Pete offered.

"Thanks, Pete," Yogi said as he turned and

walked out. Why would Buford have a special interest in that file? He wondered. Yogi checked the knob to Buford's office door but it was locked tight.

CHAPTER 23

Henry Chen was the first to find Woody German unconscious and taped to his desk chair. Using a pair of scissors he found on Woody's desk Henry cut away the tape and eased Woody back onto his bed. Woody's face was swollen, red and caked with blood. His shirt was also wet with blood that had trickled down from his nose and mouth. His left hand looked misshapen. Using a wet wash rag Henry carefully wiped blood off Woody's face. He didn't see any cuts but Woody's nose was not in the right place since part of it pointed at Woody's left ear. Woody moaned if Henry got close to his nose with the rag or if he happened to touch his left hand. Since Henry's impulse was to get help or call an ambulance, he got up from the bed just as Woody said, "Henry, Henry..." his voice weak and raspy.

"What in the hell happened to you," asked Henry.

"Henry, calling the Donovan sisters was a bad idea. Their father sent a couple of guys to send us a message," Woody struggled with speaking and moaned again.

"Hey, we need to get you to the hospital, dude," Henry said.

"Yeah, I guess so, but," Woody scratched out a few more words, "tell the guys to stop calling the Donovan girls, and the other girls as well. These guys mean business. Our war plan just blew up on us."

"Not entirely, Woody, not entirely," said Henry who was calling for an ambulance as he walked out into the hallway toward the back steps leading to the path that would take him over to the science building and the computer lab.

As an honor student Henry had his own key to the computer lab. At this time of night there was no one else in the lab which housed a very large and powerful machine. Since the forestry department was undertaking research on the pine bark beetle and kudzu for the federal government, Uncle Sam had provided a grant that paid for most of the equipment. Henry used the flashlight app on his cell phone to cross the lab to an obscure desk in one corner. The screen lit up with the dull palate of the Old Gypsy. Quickly Henry's fingers raced over the keyboard until he hit a new screen bathing Henry's face in the shimmer of colors from the screen saver of the University Bell Tower on a glorious spring day.

Good, he thought. They had not yet broken into his virus program. He decided to place more boulders in the way of his pursuers. First, if they got through the image of the Old Gypsy woman, password "Silver bullet", they would then crash into a picture of actor Rob Schneider in a hot tub with a black pimp from *Deuce Bigelow* (well recognized as one of the funniest films ever made), password "Mangina". After that, if they penetrated even further, the next image was of Alex Karras from

Blazing Saddles, password: mondolikecandy, then an image of John Belushi and Dan Akroyd from *The Blues Brothers,* password rollingrollingrolling. That ought to keep them busy for awhile, he thought confidently. He was not ready for Operation Jock Itch to be over just yet. No one would notice that the server was back up for a few minutes this late at night. Finished, he restored the image of the Old Gypsy and secured the program.

Henry chuckled to himself as he locked up and shuffled down the hall back out of the building. He didn't see Professor Jones sitting in his car in the shadow of an old oak watching as Henry left the building and passed into the shadows towards his dorm.

CHAPTER 24

On Friday Mr. Norman our IT manager called me with the first good news I had heard in the journey to restore our computer network.

"Dean, we have run a number of possible passwords trying to figure out how to get into the virus application, " he said, "Your hunch about *The Wolfman* was spot on. I tried "LonChaney", "LonChaneyjr", "werewolf", "wolf'sbane", "Larrytalbot", "gypsy", "mariaouspenskaya" and about a dozen other variations until finally we ran your guess of "silverbullet" and it worked. We were able to get inside the program."

"Great," I said, "how long before we are back up?"

"I am afraid it's not that easy. Once we got past the old gypsy we had a second surprise. Have you looked at your screen lately?" he asked.

"Not today. I got tired of the old woman staring at me, " I said as I punched the "on" button. The gypsy with those eyes was gone, but this image was a white guy and a black guy in a hot tub. I said," so, there's a second level of code to get through?"

"Yes. We have been able to identify that shot from the movie *Deuce Bigelow*. It's a great comic classic but we have got to start all over searching for passwords. If you get any inspiration let me know," Norman said.

"I'll think about it. Is there any reason to believe there are even more layers to penetrate after *Deuce Bigelow*?" I asked.

Norman said, "There's just no way to tell until we get there. We have a team working 24/7 on it."

I thanked him as I hung up. I looked up to see Tom Savage knocking on my half open door.

"Come on in Mr. Savage. What have you got?" I asked.

Savage began, "Jim Wombat showed back up. He was abducted by two guys in a Lincoln then dropped off on the old gravel road about two thirds of the way down the back of campus. He must have walked for miles, spent a night in the woods, and then caught a ride up the mountain."

I asked, "Is he ok?" I couldn't see Wombat on an extended hike.

Savage answered, "He's pretty tired, thinks he has pneumonia, and is having back pain if he walks more than a couple of steps. Plus, he has to stay close to a toilet. Seems he ate something he found in the woods and it has set him free. I think he'll be ok but he is sure motivated to find out what is going on. The guys in the car wanted to know all about the "gypsies". Wombat said they were dressed in dark suits, dark ties, sunglasses and hats."

I mused, "dark suit, dark tie, sunglasses, hat and a Lincoln. Sounds to me like Joliet Jake."

"What?" Savage asked.

"Sorry, before your time."

"Wombat thinks they are pretty serious guys. They wanted to know who was the leader of the gypsies now. Since Anderson was in the hospital, Wombat told them Woody German was in charge."

"As I recall Mr. Savage you are on the Discipline Committee aren't you?" I asked. He nodded.

"I am going to designate the hearing Monday as a joint meeting of the Executive Committees of the Discipline Committee and the Honor Council. I think issues may come up that fall within the jurisdiction of each group. Would you tell your Chairman so we can coordinate that?" I asked.

"Of course," Savage said getting up to leave. Just then Tammy Allgood came in the door and said, "Dean Mathews, we have just gotten a report of another student beat up and at the hospital."

I rubbed my temples, "who this time?" I asked.

"The student's name is Woody German, " said Mrs. Allgood.

I looked over at Savage. "Dammit," I said grabbing my hat and coat for another trip to the ER.

This time I drove out to the hospital. Nurse Garland was at the nursing station as I came through the automatic doors. "Good afternoon, Ms.

Garland," I said, "I understand you have admitted another one of my students."

She looked up but didn't smile. "Dean Mathews, we received a call and dispatched the ambulance to campus where our EMT's picked up a student named Woody German. He has been beat up pretty badly. Broken nose, bruised face, but the worst is that his left hand has been crushed as if someone slammed it in a car door. There are multiple broken bones and fragments. We are prepping him for transport to Vanderbilt for reconstructive surgery since what he needs is far beyond our ability to handle."

I wasn't smiling either. I said, "Do you know how he incurred these injuries? Did he report anything?"

She said, "No. He was conscious when he came in and could talk but he said very little. Soon after he arrived we had him so heavily sedated he became very drowsy."

I asked, because I had to, "Is there any way I could see him?"

She glared at me with a look that communicated I had just asked the stupidest question she had heard all day. "I told you that boy is hurt and sedated. Leave him alone." I nodded as Nurse Garland went back to her paperwork. I had been dismissed.

CHAPTER 25

A bright sun had burned away the fog and the morning promised to be a wonderful early spring day on the mountain. It was on such days that Yogi and I had often run Clear Creek or the Emory River Canyon in our open canoes with our friends from the Tennessee Scenic Rivers Association. The Cracker Barrel restaurant at Exit 317 off I-40 at Crossville was the usual point of rendezvous on Saturday and Sunday mornings. Trips formed up, boats were consolidated onto fewer vehicles, a destination was chosen and we took off for the put in. Most of our boats, PFD's and jackets were well worn but retained the vibrant reds, yellows, blues and greens that made it spectacular to observe twenty or so canoes and kayaks launch. My own canoe was purple. In winter and spring the Plateau creeks and rivers were full of water making the runs challenging. By reading the Oakdale Gauge maintained by TVA we could reasonably predict water levels and head off to a stream with plenty of action. Yogi and I often came to the rendezvous on the back roads past Watts Bar, Spring City, up the mountain and through Grassy Cove to the Cracker Barrel avoiding all interstates.

Today, however, I would not be heading off on a paddling trip. Yogi and I had not spoken since our last conversation about Anderson's computer. Tomorrow, the first meeting of the joint Discipline and Honor Council Executive Committees would take place and I needed to get prepared for that. So Rocket and I began our day with a run that led through a public wildflower garden where we hooked up with the footpath that followed the perimeter along the bluff that contained the campus. Rocket naturally led the way with me jogging behind at a moderate pace. Long strides were not wise on this narrow path where a misstep could send you over the bluff and down a hundred feet. Bird's Foot Violets and trillium were beginning to appear in the mossy areas of the right bank. After a couple of miles we left the trail as it passed Grandview overlook and followed gravel roads leading back toward campus. Once we were off the narrow path we picked up speed passing clumps of glorious viburnum bushes that had just begun to open filling the air with a wonderful aroma I always associated with early spring.

Back at my house there was just enough time to clean up and fix a huge breakfast for the eight students who would be arriving shortly. Eggs were scrambled, bacon was frying, biscuits were changing to that golden color when the first knock came at the door. I stepped from the kitchen long enough to let the first group of students in. Rocket was our official greeter and she was excited beyond control with so many new people who had obviously dropped by just in order to play with her. They quickly helped me lay out food family style on a side table. Within minutes everyone had arrived, picked up a plate, poured orange juice or coffee and were lustily eating a home cooked meal. It was tradition that faculty often entertained students in their homes as I had spent many hours listening to classical music in the residence of Dr.

Garrison when I was such a student. A home cooked meal was a treasure.

I knew the President of the Honor Council, Mr. Crawford, and the Chairman of the Discipline Committee, Ben Ray. They introduced the vice-chairmen and other members of their committees. Mug in hand I encouraged them to find a chair or a place on the floor of my living room and I prepared to discuss the beginning of the formal process that would start tomorrow as we attempted to resolve the issues that had erupted when the *Purple Onion* printed Anderson's letter and he was later kidnapped. Impressively, there were four men and four women looking at me. In addition to the officers, each of the Committees had selected a special investigator who were not present. The special investigator collected the evidence and presented the case to the Executive Committee. The action recommended by the Executive Committees would determine whether or not a hearing was conducted before the full Committee of each group. Each committee had twelve members: four seniors, four juniors, three sophomores, and one freshman.

I began, "Thank you for agreeing to share your Sunday morning with me. Each of you has an important role in the conduct of student life on this campus. As incoming freshmen you each signed off that you would abide by the Honor Code, which has been one of the foundations of this school for over a century. This Code provides the framework which creates our community of honor and respect.

Nothing is more fundamental to our value system than honor. It cannot be defined except in the broadest of terms yet it permeates all we do, all we are, and all we will become. A person without honor is to be society's outcast and vilified as unworthy. Honor lives in the soul of this place and in every student's heart. To be without honor is to be without the bread of life. Over the past few weeks our honor has been challenged." I paused to confirm I had captured my audience. No one was crying, but a damn good opening statement, I thought.

So, I went on, "We are now presented with multiple issues of misconduct which can only be described as dishonorable. We cannot tolerate some of the things that have happened in recent days. Since each of you wears the mantle of the code of honor, it falls on you to take action. As Associate Dean I am here to help you in any way that I can, but ultimately, the role you play is primary, and much more important than mine." A few were beginning to squirm.

I said, "As I see it we have the following matters that you need to address: One (as I held up one finger) Was Bob Anderson telling the truth when he said he had cheated on all his exams? Two, did he actually see others cheat, and who? Three, what happened to Anderson the night he was abducted? Four, what should be done about the puke in the purse? Five, what about the assault on the student outside the Sigma Delta house? And finally, Six, What has happened to our computer system and is a student or group of students involved in that?" I didn't even go into anything else we had been dealing with such as the drugs, the guys in the Lincoln, or the Mexicans. If I tried to think about all of it at once my head might just explode.

Clendon Crawford spoke first saying "as to the first item, whether Anderson told the truth or was lying, or cheated, or saw anyone else cheat will have to wait until his health improves, so I think we can shelve that for awhile. We cannot engage in any kind of hearings without the person charged being present." Mr. Crawford knew his procedure and expressed a sense of fairness. Most of the students nodded although Ben Ray was very still.

Crawford went on, "Our investigator has spoken with a number of students and is prepared to present information tomorrow regarding Anderson's abduction. We also have credible information regarding the purse incident but nothing on the Sigma Delta assault." Crawford clearly had access to some information that was not known to all present, including me. I gave him a look that said he had better be prepared to show me his cards before tomorrow.

"Does anyone have anything on the Sigma Delta incident? "asked Ben Ray. When no one spoke up he continued, "Then our Executive Committee will likely recommend that matter be closed."

Clendon Crawford then asked, "Ben you are a member of that fraternity, don't you think maybe you are a little too close to the action here?"

Ben Ray locked eyes with Crawford and said very deliberately, "If there's no proof, there's no proof and it is a waste of time here before finals and comprehensive exams for the seniors."

Crawford met the stare and said, "I am not sure what's going on here, Ben."

The two of them were eyeing each other like Bighorn sheep preparing to crack skulls when Judy Travers, the Honor Council vice-chair said, " Dean Mathews, I know that the school has been working on the computer issue. What's the status of that? Are exams in jeopardy of being delayed?"

Thankful she had changed the subject, if only slightly, I told them our team had cracked the Wolfman code only to find the picture from *Deuce Bigelow* exposed. I said, "If any of you have any suggestions please let us know. The link is not as clear with this one as it was to the word "gypsy" with the first image."

That's when the chatter in the room picked up and that's when Charlie Sims from the Discipline Committee said, "I know that movie. My roommate watches it so much he has memorized most of the lines. In that scene the pimp is explaining to Deuce how he can become a "man-whore" with his "mangina". While the guys laughed, the girls in the room were embarrassed and clearly not as taken with the movie as some of the guys. Things were starting to deteriorate, and I knew we had done about all we could until tomorrow.

I said, "You know what you need to do. I have reserved the Trustee's Board room for 7pm tomorrow. Normally, these meetings would be closed but there have been several inquiries about this so I am inclined to let the meeting be open. Just remember we all have to respect the privacy rights of anyone who may have been involved or a witness to anything. Save actual names until afterwards and report them to me."

We said our goodbye's and the students peeled out into the warm Sunday sunshine. Mr. Crawford turned to me as the last to leave and said, "Dean, with email being down I couldn't keep you up to date as much as I would like to but I will call you later if that's ok?" I assured him it would be fine and closed the door. I immediately called Mr. Norman with the suggestion regarding "man-whore" and "mangina". Since he was at his computer, he tried both and yelled "Bingo". Then he said "Oh, shit. What do you know about *Blazing Saddles*?" I told him I would get back to him as I turned on my laptop to the picture of Alex Karras.

A few minutes later as I cleaned up the dishware, President Callicott called and asked about the committee meetings. He planned to attend perhaps with a guest. His voice was very icy and sharp. If everything went sideways I did not think I could count on the President to have my back.

CHAPTER 26

Emily Sellars met me at the quad with a day pack and we decided to head off the mountain to hike the Fiery Gizzard Trail. I was not sure how this creek that bounded down sculpted rocks for miles until it leapt over a forty foot waterfall into a crystal pool had gotten its name. Perhaps from the Cherokee who had lived in this area. Rocket bounced around the back seat of my Jeep and licked Emily who had climbed into the passenger side in a seat normally reserved for Rocket who was convinced she was a front seat dog. As Rocket and Emily wrestled between the seats, I eased onto University Avenue and headed down the mountain to the trailhead parking lot. The trail itself follows Fiery Gizzard Creek as it meanders through a rhododendron and Hemlock forest. It's an easy hike with numerous ups and downs but you must exercise a degree of care since the path crosses tree roots and rocks and a misstep could mean a quick plunge into the rushing water or even worse bounce down jagged rocks. When I was in school we had to wade from one side to the other in order to continue following the trail, but today the State had constructed a couple of foot bridges that made the traverse so much simpler. The old route was more fun.

On the way to our lunch stop, I reached down and pulled up a stem which I scraped with my thumb until it was a bright yellow color staining my fingers in the process.

"This, young lady, is yellow root which the Indians used for war paint," I said showing off my knowledge of the woods in an attempt to impress my date. Just call me Natty Bumpo.

In turn Emily pulled up a small plant and said "and this is pipsissewa or spearmint whose scientific name is *Chimaphila umbellata*. Indians used this as flavoring." Touche. This girl likely knew a whole lot more botany than me so I decided not to show off exactly how little I knew. Yellow root was about it.

The air under the hemlocks was fresh and cool. Everything was moist enhancing not only the growth of moss on the rocks but also the slippery factor of the rocks and roots. After about a mile we came to a waterfall that looked perfect to Rocket since it fell over a ten foot rock outcropping into a clear pool. Climbing down to the lower pool, Emily and I sat at the edge of the pool with our bare feet in the water as Rocket swam circles wondering why that tail thing was following her. Emily's long and gorgeous legs and such pretty feet stretched into the pool and she said, "What do you think is going to happen with all this mess at school?"

I thought for a second trying to get my mind around all the parts of the "mess". "We may never know the truth about everything. The students are not talking. I think there is some information the Honor Council has found out about the truck and who arranged for its use, but beyond that I'm looking into an empty sack. Once we get the server back up we might be able to trace who is behind that." I looked over at her as she lounged head back, eyes closed, raven hair all over her bare shoulders, and those legs! Delicious.

"What really bothers me is that things over which we have no control keep happening. There are outside forces involved. This is not just about The Red Dagger Society or Bob Anderson. I assume there have been no more calls to the girls?" I asked.

Without opening her eyes, Emily said, "No. That stopped abruptly and I have heard no more complaints, thank goodness."

"Do you know why they stopped?" I asked.

"No. Do you?"

"What I've heard is that two big guys in a Lincoln came onto campus and paid a visit to one of the gypsies, Woody German, after which Mr. German went to the hospital for surgery to his hand and the calls stopped," I offered.

Emily sat up and said, "You're kidding me, right?"

"Nope. Straight out of *The Godfather*," I said. "And, then three Mexicans showed up at my house and borrowed Mr. Anderson's laptop computer," I added.

Emily's turquois eyes flashed as she queried, "Borrowed?"

I said, "Euphemistically speaking. They blew a hole in my floor with a pistol and I handed it over."

"Holy, shit," Emily said. "Did you report it?"

"I was warned not to. Besides, only one person knew I even had that laptop. Yogi," I said.

"Son of a bitch. You don't think Yogi's involved do you?" Emily asked. I liked it when girls cussed and she could do it with such passion.

I said, "I know he has kept his distance from me the last few days, but he handed me the laptop when he got it from Anderson's girlfriend. I just don't know what to think or who I can trust."

Emily's hand gently touched my forearm the electricity arcing through me like a Tesla globe. "You can trust me, Jack," she said looking into the water and moving slightly closer.

I said, "I know." My toes caressed the top of her foot and when I leaned into the shimmer of her eyes we kissed for the first time. Slow and measured. My heart was racing and I wanted more. Emily's kiss was one of wonder and exploration. Tentative at first, on my second try she was into the passion as was I. When we came up for air, I put the daypack behind my head and rocked back. She snuggled into my chest purring.

For a long time I lay on my back with

Emily's head on my chest my arm around her shoulders. My heart was thundering in my chest. Her hair smelled like apricots and I couldn't get enough of her scent. I wanted to caress her and move forward, but this feeling with her was so new I was afraid to be more aggressive. On the other hand, I thought, perhaps she wants me to make the next move. Maybe she wants me to be more aggressive, have a little lust in my heart. In the swirl of this doubt neither of us spoke and the muffled roar of the waterfall was hypnotic. I had not felt like this in a long time since I had been too busy with advancing my career. The calmness covered us like a blanket. I now realized my attraction to Emily had become an irresistible force that I could not deny. I wanted to speak but I also did not want this moment interrupted by anything. There was a lot more I wanted to learn about this girl. I wanted to explore her nature and I wanted her to look at me and think "ok" this is the guy, the guy I could cherish for the rest of my life. I wanted her to be mine, and me hers. I looked up and imagined we were soaring with wings through the puffy clouds dipping and rising and carving next to heaven. All I could see were the white whispery clouds passing overhead visible only through the opening in the forest canopy created by the presence of Gizzard Creek and the rock formations. All I could hear was the roar of the waterfall and the thumping of our hearts.

Only Rocket's cycle of swim-shake off-lay down-then start all over again provided any distraction. Being here with Emily was good. It felt right. When Rocket had finally bored of the pool she came over and plopped down next to me her damp side in contrast to the warmth of Emily on the other. There we lay for the longest time suspended in time and space.

Finally Emily asked, "Why did you come back?" She and I had been at the college at the same time but hardly knew each other then. She was raised up on one elbow her fingers still caressing my chest.

"Because I thought I could make a difference. I thought I could help, " I said my fingers moving through her hair like playing with fine strands of silk.

"What about you," I asked.

"It's what I thought I would always do. I love this place. I grew up on a college campus with my parents and it all seems so natural to me. I love the Oxford like feel of the place and even the Westminster chimes ringing every fifteen minutes," answered Emily. Her hand rested against my chest and occasionally her fingers stretched out touching Rocket's damp side that rose and fell as she twitched dreaming in the pursuit of something. A few more minutes of silence passed.

Emily raised up again her turquois eyes piercing into my almost closed lids. "We should be getting back before it gets dark," she said and kissed me lightly. I didn't want to move but she was right. Without flashlights we did not want to be navigating this rocky trail in the dark.

At the top of the trailhead parking lot I toweled off Rocket who had splashed into and out of the creek several times heading back. Rocket hopped into the back seat settled down with a grunt. She was one tired pup. By the time I hit the paved road she would be asleep. I drove back up the mountain using my left hand, since I was holding Emily's hand in my right one and I didn't want to let go. We talked of the old days at school of old teachers and friends, those that had grown and those that had were trapped in the amber of college years and would forever remain the same. Casually, we were getting to know each other. Nothing was rushed since we had all the time in the world. That's what life at this campus was like, time could be suspended.

We entered the campus on University Avenue. It occurred to me that I wasn't even sure where Emily's house was. She gave me directions and when we got there she looked again into my eyes and said teasingly, "Why don't you come in, Jack. It's been a wonderful day and I don't think I want it to be over just yet." Exactly the words I had hoped to hear. For the slightest second thoughts of all the mysteries circling around me pushed against the moment trying to gain traction once again. I shut that door in my head and smiled at Emily as Rocket and I got out of the Jeep.

CHAPTER 27

Bruce Sidwell knocked on the door to Winston Campbell's room.

"Come in," said Winston who was not expecting one of his freshman pledges at this hour. In fact he had not seen Bruce since the Deputy had escorted him away from the Kappa Zeta house.

"If it isn't Bruce the Purse. You know my boy, you are becoming quite the legend. Of course, if the Discipline Committee ever really finds out, you could be toast. What can I do for you?" asked Winston who was leaning back in his desk chair with his feet up on the desk. As a senior Winston had one of the few single rooms in the dorm and one with a private bath.

Bruce began, "The night the Deputy took me to the jail is still really fuzzy to me."

"Hell Bruce, you couldn't handle the artillery punch. I told all of you pledges to take it easy. That stuff sneaks up on you and then it's light out before you know it. You got so blasted I watched as you melted into one of the straight backed chairs along the wall. At that point I think you had already puked once. Then, and this is the god's truth, Mrs. Zimmer who is married to the French teacher came over and sat in your lap. But she was so blasted I don't think she knew you were there. You looked right at her tits and blinked," laughed Winston.

"And then, one of your contacts went right down the inside front of her dress and into her bra. I think that's when she realized where she was and jumped up just before you went hunting for the contact" Winston said laughing even more.

"I don't remember any of that," said Bruce sheepishly.

"Well, it happened and I was there. So, what's up now?" asked Winston.

"I have gotten into something and I don't know what to do," said Bruce. Winston lowered his legs and turned toward Bruce who was sitting in the lounge chair where Winston would often study late at night. Winston was thinking "has he knocked up some coed?" But, he would be wrong.

Bruce went on, "They kept me in that jail for two days. On the day I was to get out a Mexican guy came into the cell and sat next to me on the cot. He told me that he had a proposition for me that could mean a lot of money. He asked me a bunch of questions and said that he was in need of someone to assist him with the distribution of certain drugs. Mostly speed but some harder stuff on occasion." Winston was listening closely because he believed Bruce was telling him the truth about what happened. He just couldn't believe what he was hearing.

"Did you ask him why he was talking to you?" asked Winston.

"Yeah," said Bruce. "He said his current agent had left school."

"You mean Anderson?" asked Winston.

"No, his roommate. The guy that split after Anderson was found in front of the Union." Bruce continued, "He told me I would keep half from the sale of each pill, and a flat fee each time I made a pick up and delivery. He said I could make a few thousand dollars each month."

Winston said, "Wow. You know that's illegal as hell. You don't want to get messed up with a drug dealer. Why don't you just tell him no?"

" Because I'm scared. The whole time he was sitting in my cell he had a knife he was using to clean his finger nails. Every now and then he pointed it at me, and said how he did not like people who disappointed him, and then he pulled out a stack of photographs," said Bruce.

"What kind of photos, Bruce," Winston asked.

"Photographs of fingers, just fingers, and hands with no fingers, and an arm with no hand at all, "Bruce was about to cry. "What kind of shit have I gotten into?" Bruce asked.

"So you came to me," Winston said.

"That's why I am here, Winston. I don't know what to do. I am supposed to meet this guy again in a couple of days to seal the arrangement and make the first pickup," pleaded Bruce.

"Let me think about it. I may be able to come up with something that helps us all. It may be time to start trading," said Winston. "Don't say anything else to anyone. "

After Bruce left Winston dialed his cousin Braxton' cell phone. Braxton had been the leader of the Red Dagger while a student and still remained connected. Although Braxton was in Marine Corps Officer Training at Marine Corps Base Quantico, it was late evening and he picked up the call after only a couple of rings.

Winston said, "Braxton how's it going?"

"Not too bad, although at the moment the weather is so bad the Base is at Red Flag so there's not much going on outside," Braxton offered.

"You holding up ok?" asked Winston.

Braxton said, "I used to think football practice was tough with all the shit Coach Boothead made us do, but that ain't nothing compared to this."

"The few, the brave, the proud," said Winston.

"Yep. Did you guys take care of that pussy we talked about? I hope this story doesn't start with but first we took our clothes off" Braxton said.

Winston said, "No, not one of those stories.

We took care of it. Almost too good. The little shit is in the hospital in a coma. I don't know what went on that night but the guys assure me they just fucked with him for a few hours, scared the shit out of him, then deposited him back on campus in the truck dressed up like the corn flakes duck just as you suggested."

Braxton laughed. "Wish I could have seen that, man do I wish I could have seen that."

"You would have been proud of us, Cuz, but that's not why I'm calling. We have something more serious going on and I need your advice," Winston began.

"Shoot, daddy rabbit," Braxton said.

"It looks like the punk we snatched was actually a dope and pills dealer for a bunch of Mexicans who have now contacted one of our new pledges and are trying to coerce him into being their new mule," Winston said.

"You're shitting me, right?" Braxton fired back.

"Nope, god's truth. My pledge is pretty scared and he thinks these Mexicans mean business. You got any suggestions about our next move," asked Winston.

"We've got the FBI facility right here on base. Want me to tip them off?" Braxton offered.

Winston said, "Hold onto that idea, but it

might be overkill if we have federal agents crawling all over this place."

"Okay, your call," said Braxton."You probably don't know this, but one of our old Red Dagger members was from the area and I think is now a deputy in the sheriff's department."

Winston said, "Do you mean Deputy Yogi Baker?"

Braxton agreed, "Yep. He's a good man, part of the GMF squad. I think you can trust him. I also heard the President brought back that guy Mathews as Associate Dean. I have heard he's a stand up guy as well. Why don't you lay it out for these guys and get them involved before it blows out of control."

"Thanks, Cuz," Winston said continuing, "You know the Red Dagger will help any way we can but this may be over our heads."

"Call that deputy and talk to the Dean. Gotta run, they are blowing taps on my ass. Talk to you later bud." And with that Braxton disconnected. A plan was coming together in Winston's head.

CHAPTER 28

When Jim Wombat caught the scent of a story he followed the trail to ground. The fact that he had been snatched and left in the woods added to his motivation to figure out what was going on. Like the rest of school his ability to access email was halted as was the printing of the *Purple Onion.* However, Wombat could still write the stories and wait for the presses to roll again. With each hour that passed he wrote and rewrote articles adding more color each time he discovered something new. Although a copy editor would normally compose a story's headline he was composing titillating ones in his head such as "Thugs invade campus" and "Red Dagger Hires Hitmen", and the like. Whether his Editor would ever allow such captions, he did not know.

He had heard that the Honor Council investigator had a lead to someone who had seen the person who took the University truck. This was the first break in the Red Dagger case. That information would be laid out at the Executive Committee meetings tonight and Jim planned to be there. Instinctively, he knew that somehow Henry Chen was involved in the computer breakdown so he looked for Henry around campus until he found him in the computer lab early on Monday morning.

"Okay, Henry. Tell me what you are up to. I know you have something to do with the hack of the University server. I can tell you the administration and the President are out to catch whoever is involved. And, when they do it won't be pretty," Wombat said.

Henry rolled around in the chair and nodded. He knew it was time for this to end and Jim was his best friend. He said, "It may have gone too far. When Bob was taken and hurt we decided on a war plan called Operation Jock Itch. It was just supposed to be a little fun or at least that's how we planned it. Then somebody got to Woody and hurt him bad. Woody told us all to back off. I just couldn't believe how badly Woody was torn up."

Wombat had already told Henry about the guys in the Lincoln who left him in the woods and that he had given them Woody's name. Henry wasn't blaming Jim. "Let me help you get out of this now," said Wombat. "If we can restore the computer system, I can tell the Dean that you provided me with information trying to help. I will assure him you are not involved and maybe they will be so relieved they will look the other way."

Henry was not sure this plan would work but he was tired and ready for it to be over. He said, "The computer image now playing is a picture of Alex Karras from *Blazing Saddles.* Karras is the former NFL player turned actor who plays "Mongo" in that movie."

Wombat said, "Yep. Now give me two possible passwords, one of which is the real password, assuming of course, you have an idea what it is."

"Tell the Dean to try "YesNo" and "Mongolikecandy"," said Henry.

"What does "YesNo" mean," Wombat asked.

"That was tattooed on the Ox's butt that Mongo rode into town on," said Henry.

"And the other is a famous line from the movie?" asked Jim.

"Yes," said Henry. "Then, give them "Aretha" and "RollingRollingRolling".

"There's more?" asked Jim.

"The last one is a shot of John Belushi and Dan Akroyd from *The Blues Brothers* dressed like the guys who grabbed you, " said Henry.

Wombat told Henry to stay cool and headed directly to the Dean's Office.

CHAPTER 29

I had just sat down at my desk when I heard the office door open. Emily popped her head into my office, smiled and waived. I waived back as she hummed all the way into her space. This felt good. My heart jumped with a passion for her. Sometimes all it took was a glance or a waive of the hand. Images from the prior evening began to creep back into my head like smoke through a keyhole when Jim Wombat's face appeared in the doorway jerking me back into the present and ruining my daydream. With all I had to worry about, Emily's distraction was most welcome. She was the only bright star I could see. Mr. Wombat's appearance however, spun me back into the swirling chaos and all we had to figure out to restore order at the school. I also knew that time was running out, a point made clear by the President when we had last spoken. His tolerance for the quagmire that engulfed the school had grown thin.

"Dean Mathews, I have some information that may help get the server back on line," Wombat said puffing as he acquired the seat across from my desk. He had apparently taken the stairs and not the elevator. Wombat was a small guy almost childlike in the high backed chair.

"You have certainly got my attention, Mr. Wombat," I said as I studied the small almost gnome like student. Wombat did not like direct eye contact and try as I would I could not get him to latch onto my eyes. This conveyed the impression that perhaps he was not about to tell the truth or that he might omit some part of the truth. Wombat would get killed if he played poker.

"Sir, my roommate is Henry Chen who is pretty good with computers. He has been getting ready for finals but I asked him to help me figure out the passwords based upon the movie scenes that keep appearing on the computer screens. I am doing a story on the whole event for the paper. Between the two of us we were pretty familiar with all the movies. He suggests you try "YesNo" or "Mongolikecandy" on the picture from *Blazing Saddles.* "

I got the Mongolikecandy line but I asked " Why YesNo?"

Wombat said, "Like on the ox's butt Mongo was riding into town?"

I nodded. Then I told him not to move and called up Mr. Norman. "So try "YesNo" as a password. Doesn't work? Okay, then try "Mongolikecandy", I said. After Norman said "Bingo" he said a new image had popped up. I looked up at Wombat and said, "Now there's an image of John Belushi and Dan Akroyd with hats and sunglasses from *The Blues Brothers.* "

"Let me call Henry real quick and see what he thinks about this one," said Jim Wombat who picked up his cell phone and appeared to be punching in numbers. I listened as it sounded like he told Henry Chen about the new image. From the side of the conversation I could hear they went back and forth with several alternatives and Wombat finally hung up and said, "Try "Aretha" and "RollingRollingRolling.""

I picked back up with Mr. Norman and once again he said "Bingo" after trying "RollingRollingRolling".

"What's popped up now?" I asked.

"Nothing," said Norman, "All I see is a spring photo of the Bell Tower and now, we are back up and running."

I hung up with Mr. Norman and looked suspiciously at Jim Wombat. He gave me a pleasant smile and I said, "Mr. Wombat, you can tell Mr. Chen that while I appreciate his assistance, I am still curious how he happened to come up with the correct password twice."

"Lucky, or maybe he's a really bright guy," Wombat said taking his leave and scurrying out.

When I turned on my machine I logged in for the first time in days to be greeted by the Bell Tower image someone had chosen as the default screen saver. I watched patiently as my computer loaded several days' worth of emails when the phone rang. It was Special Agent Bradley.

"Dean Mathews," SA Bradley said, "our TBI lab has confirmed the pills are a form of amphetamine known in the trade as "speed" or

"Black Beauties". They are very popular on college campuses especially around exam time. A student can pop one of these and study straight through 24 or 48 hours before an exam. Every time he drinks a Coca-Cola the buzz recharges. The problem we have is that these pills are contaminated with minute traces of a drug called alpha-Pyrrolidinopentiophenone. In street talk it is known as "flakka". Pretty bad stuff that puts the user into a state called "excited delirium". I have spoken with the Feds and they have traced this contaminant to a pharmaceutical plant in Mexico. The effect of the contaminant is to induce hallucinations, paranoia, coma and even death. We tested several of the pills and they all hit on positive for this contaminant."

I was stunned. This could explain Anderson's condition at the hospital. But, how many of these damn pills were loose on campus? I asked, "Have you checked with the hospital on Bob Anderson's bloodwork?"

"Yes, that's why I am calling. His bloodwork is positive for this same chemical. It now looks like his condition is a reaction to this chemical rather than the hazing," Bradley said.

I thanked him for the call and wondered how was I going to alert any student who may have done business with Anderson? I quickly dialed Mr. Norman in the Information Technology Office.

"Is there any way that I can get an emergency message out to everyone on campus?

We have a potential health situation developing," I said.

Mr. Norman answered, "With enough time we could write a program that texted every student with a cell phone and simultaneously hit everyone's email. It would take some time to write the code that would capture all the cell numbers and email addresses from administrative records but we are covered up just trying to restore our systems and applications. This is a project I had planned on implementing this semester when everything fell off the table. Of course if we had some help…"

I broke in, "You mean from someone who was a gifted code writing computer whiz?"

"Yes, he said. Who do you have in mind?" asked Mr. Norman.

"How about Henry Chen?" I offered.

"Henry would be great but I doubt we could persuade him to interrupt studying for finals and comps," Norman said.

"Let me see if I can convince him," I said.

By now Tammy was at her desk. I yelled through the open door, "Call Jim Wombat's cell phone and tell him to bring Henry Chen here immediately."

"Yes sir," Tammy said.

Twenty minutes later both Jim and Henry

were in my office. I rose, shut the door and sat on the edge of my desk looking down at the two of them in the chairs Emily and I had been sitting in when this all started. For a minute I just stared at them as I leaned back on the desk letting them squirm.

"Gentlemen, we are facing a very serious situation. The authorities have told me that drugs were seized in Mr. Anderson's dorm room which contain a chemical traced to a Mexican pharmaceutical plant. This chemical is so dangerous it can induce a coma in anyone who comes into contact with it, or even death. We do not know how widespread the contaminated pills are or how many are in circulation but we need to respond quickly."

I continued, "I asked you to come here because I need a favor. Henry, your computer skills are well known to Mr. Norman in our Information Technology Office. We need your assistance to send a text and email blast to every student warning that no one should use any pills or other drugs they acquired from another student or anyone else. I am sure this will consume time you would want to spend getting ready for exams and comps, but as I said I need a favor. In return I am prepared to do you a favor."

Henry nodded still mute and I continued, "I think it is very coincidental that you were so quickly able to provide accurate passwords to break the lock into our server when Mr Norman and his staff were unable to do so. It has also come to my attention that you have been seen late at night at the computer lab in the last few days as our server was being hacked into. One coincidence is hard for me to accept but two coincidences just don't happen." I just stared at him trying not to blink and pausing as if it were his turn to speak. I had learned this device from a law school course I had taken once regarding depositions of witnesses. Most people could not resist the natural tendency to fill up empty space with talk. While Wombat was looking anywhere but at me, Henry's eyes locked on mine and he knew that I knew.

"I understand Dean Mathews. How can I help?" asked Henry.

"Good. I am prepared to overlook any involvement you may have had into what happened to our computer system, if you get your skinny ass down to the lab now and send out these messages. Mr. Wombat is here to witness that we have an understanding," I said handing the typed messages to Wombat. Henry glanced at the paper and its simple message. Then he looked up at me. Without much hesitation he responded having instantly grabbed for the rescue rope I had tossed in his direction.

"Yes Sir," said Henry as he and Wombat bolted out of my office. Although I was positive Mr. Chen had something to do with the hacking of our server, the safety of students overrode any desire for punishment. If Henry Chen could pull this off quickly, I would owe him the favor. I was mentally checking off the targets one by one.

My phone rang and it was one of a group of students I had met when we began to reorganize the paddling club. She introduced herself as Joan Ward.

"Dean Mathews, a few of the paddling club members would like to get out today and paddle something, are you up for it?" she asked with an enticing lilt in her voice. As the weather had warmed we were beginning to see the first of a series of weeks where the creeks and rivers were full and offered an opportunity to paddle interesting waters that would vanish in a couple of months. I had been so engrossed in the issues at school I had almost forgotten my commitment to the club so I was primed for a getaway.

"We would have to hit something close," I said.

She said "There's about ten who want to get out and do something. Everybody is going stir crazy."

"Tell you what," I said, imagining we could get to the West Fork of the Obey in about an hour and a half, "get everyone over to the storage room, pick out boats and all the gear and I will meet you there in a few minutes. This is going to be an open boat trip so leave the kayaks. I need to run home and get my stuff."

"Great," she said and hung up.

I had thrown together impromptu trips like this before, but my biggest concern was the experience level of this group. We had taken one trip to the Nantahala River in late fall and I had not been overly impressed with the skill level of these kids. They had all the flexibility of youth and the desire for adventure. A technical stream like the West Fork could be a challenge but the school of hard knocks could teach many life lessons and this stream had only one truly punishing rapid. I would need some support, and since Yogi and I seemed to be somewhat estranged I speed dialed my buddy Mike who lived near the West Fork. Mike was ready to paddle anywhere anytime. He said he would check the gauge at the take out bridge and meet me at the put in by noon. I checked in with Emily and told her I would be back late.

At the paddling storage room gear was already laid out and in the process of being sorted by the time I arrived. After we made sure everyone had a personal flotation device, or lifejacket as they were sometimes called, and a spare paddle for the open boats, we lifted and loaded on top of the cars tying to the roof racks with a trucker's hitch that enabled a single rope to cinch tight against itself. Our parade of three cars presented a colorful array of boats mounted on drab colored vehicles. Although I insisted that real paddlers knew how to handle an open boat this was becoming more and more the exception as kayaks dominated. They were simpler vessels and if you had perfected a roll, the chances of swimming sans boat were reduced. Real open boaters, however, could "roll" even a canoe. At one time I had used that maneuver to impress lady paddlers, until one of them showed me how graceful a roll could be executed by a woman who used skill instead of muscle to make the turn.

The excitement of a new river energized these paddlers. The challenge of the unknown usually produced a rush of adrenaline. A particularly attractive blonde girl climbed into the front passenger seat of my Jeep and flashed a big smile. Hello, darling.

Two lane back roads cut deep through the mountain and then the Sequatchie Valley as we climbed up to the Plateau towards Livingston in Overton County. To access the West Fork we had to park near a cemetery off a country lane where the oldest headstones were carved into a rounded replica of a human torso. Someone had explained to me that those stones were a holdover from immigrants who had come to this area from Celtic lands in Europe two centuries earlier. As we unloaded the boats and piled loose gear into the vessels Mike arrived and said the gauge on the take out bridge was running about six feet which was a very manageable level. Much below that level and the stream became too rocky and much higher meant a very technical pushy run that I was not sure this crew was ready for.

The West Fork of the Obey is one of the very special Plateau streams where fourteen waterfalls pour into the river. If you hit the season right as wildflowers appeared both sides of the river were painted with every hue of natural colors. As the drivers ran a shuttle back to the take out the others drug the boats down to the edge of the river waiting for us to return. The slogan was always, beer and keys at the bottom. This was a paddler's version of "be prepared". Losing keys on a run, or having to wait on beer until the shuttle was completed was a real downer. If the shuttle were done right only one car would be left at the put in.

All geared up with pfd's, helmets, inflated air bags in the boats, and the appropriate rescue gear, I gave my routine paddling safety talk emphasizing that Mike would run lead and I would be the sweep. No one ran in front of Mike or behind me for obvious reasons. Even though all of these paddlers had been on rivers before, primarily the Hiwassee, a narrow Plateau stream like this one that was choked full of boulders presented a different challenge because it was important to be able to slow up, stop or catch an eddy to scout a line through an unfamiliar rapid. Charging headlong into the unknown was a good way to get hurt or go swimming and the water temperature was still cold this time of year.

I explained that boat control was all important, to stay out of strainers, or piles of brush or trees that may have caught on the side of the river, and not to crowd other paddlers. Not running over someone in front of you who was scouting a line was especially difficult for rookie paddlers.

Saying "sorry" didn't help much in a pile up. Finally, I explained Kelsey's First Three Rules for Open Boaters: the "Wiggle Waggle", the "Twist and Shout", and the "Rock and Roll." These basic maneuvers were intended to loosen up and stretch the muscles and to remind open boaters that the paddles should be free to turn in the hand and move as you altered strokes to make the boat go where you wanted. In the middle of my lesson, youthful enthusiasm won out and I recognized I had lost my audience.

With Mike in the lead we launched into the current peeling out and to the left as the river dropped away quickly ultimately to collect in a lake miles away. Our trip would cover only about six miles leaving us near a short bridge and miles from the lake. Some of the paddlers were more vocal than others but all seemed focused on not going for a swim. Paddling an open canoe was all about balance. Leaning the boat until water was ready to pour in the gunnels was a necessary exercise and one you needed to be able to rely on if you had to carve into or out of an eddy along the way down. Lean and stroke. Staying fluid and under control was much more pleasant than the old flip and swim move.

Of the fourteen waterfalls that parade into this river, there was one in particular to watch for because it is essential to pass behind and through the waterfall to line up correctly for the rapid just below. Mike executed that move and disappeared. Then one after another of the student paddlers followed him squealing as they passed through and out the other side. We continued downstream until we found a spot where we could all pull into the same large eddy above the only named rapid on the river. This one was called "Big Mama" for a reason. The force of the stream pushed to the right around a large boulder then around and through a series of smaller boulders before dropping over a small ledge. Like a pin ball machine, water crashing off the rocks changed directions without warning requiring the paddler to execute a series of strokes and some that were not intuitive. A well executed back stroke followed by a hard pull as the current pushed the stern of the canoe to the left was essential to make the only chute, otherwise the paddler arrived broad side into another group of rocks and would be pinned or flipped. Pinning could mean the collapse of the gunnels trapping the paddler within the boat.

Mike demonstrated the proper technique and ran the line clean. Below, he was able to eddy river right and got out of his boat on a shelf where we planned to eat lunch. With his throw rope at the ready he watched from below as I observed from above when the next ten boats in a row failed to make it through. In an instant absolute chaos reigned. There were ten canoes either pinned or headed different directions and ten helmets of swimming paddlers in the water at the same time. This was a major fuck up. I paddled quickly through the chaos to river left and also jumped from my boat when I felt the bottom of my canoe scrape the bottom of the creek. I identified ten helmets in various stages of floating most of which were headed right in Mike's direction. Counting heads was my only quick and viable method to be sure someone wasn't caught beneath a boat or wedged in a rock. Using his throw rope and a paddle Mike was able to snare nine of the boaters and get them to the shelf. Only one was headed towards me, my blonde friend from the front seat. I hit her across the shoulders with the throw rope and pulled her into the eddy where I was standing, her knight in shining neoprene. I grabbed her pfd and pulled her up. First thing I had to do was to be sure she had not become hypothermic. If she started shaking I would normally have rubbed on the paddler to stimulate circulation or hug the paddler to provide warmth, or under extreme conditions take off both our clothes and crawl into a sleeping bag using my body heat to warm the victim. Somehow, I knew none of those options were going to work here. Still dripping water she turned as she stood and her lips were only inches from mine. She smiled and gave me a peck on the cheek.

"Thanks," she said.

"Thank you," I returned. Mike and I spent the next half hour unpinning and catching canoes until we had all the boats pulled up onto the shelf. We were lucky there had been no real damage, just a few more scrapes and dents. Finally, we were able to sit down and eat our sandwiches. Mike gave me a look that said "what a bunch of rookies." I just nodded. We were both exhausted. My new friend came over next to me and touched my arm all the while flashing me with that big pleasant smile. I found I was smiling back. What was going on here? I wondered. Whatever she was selling I seemed to be buying.

Only a couple of tricky bends in the river lay below Big Mama and my company made it through with flying colors. For the rest of the trip my new blonde friend was not far away and secured her seat in the front of my Jeep when we made it to the take out before anyone else could move in. Her closeness had not escaped Mike's notice either. When we finished loading the boats for home, he came around to where I was checking the last rope and said,

"Watch it big boy. I think you've got a live one there," nodding in the direction of my front seat. Oh, boy.

The lovely Miss Ward hit the play button on my audio and a CD of selected rock music blew out the speakers. First came *Sweet Home Alabama* then *Money for Nothing* and the hits kept coming. Beers were passed around and I realized we had just killed it. It had been a great afternoon and I hadn't thought about the Red Dagger crap for hours.

Back at the storage room in the rear of the Gym, Miss Ward came over and said,

"I hope to see you again, soon." I gulped as she handed me a slip of paper on which was written her cell phone number.

CHAPTER 30

Clendon Crawford entered the old administration building that was attached to the building housing most of the academic classrooms and went down a set of steps into the basement area. This part of the structure contained offices for student activities such as the *Purple Onion*, the Drama Club, and various language clubs. As expected Tom Savage was pecking away at his computer keyboard editing an article for an upcoming story.

Tom looked up and said, "Just a sec. Let me finish this edit. Seems I am having a hard time keeping a governor on Jim Wombat. Everything he turns in is related to the Red Dagger story and he is growing more and more aggressive." Completing the red line version, he saved the document and turned to Clendon.

"What's up?" he questioned.

"Do you have any idea what's really going on around here?" Clendon asked as he settled into one of the metal chairs across from Tom. They had been friends since their freshman year and could speak frankly with each other. Clendon respected Tom's insightful eye, and Tom knew Clendon was the one person who would remain true and honest in all things.

"I thought I knew, but there's a bunch of moving parts," Tom said.

"I agree. There's something else going on with this Anderson guy," Clendon said.

"What do you mean?" asked Tom.

"I was told that the Dean and two officers removed a large toolbox from Anderson's room the other night."

"Yeah. So what was in it?" Tom asked.

"Rachel, who works in the history department said something about drugs." Clendon offered.

"You mean that pretty secretary?" Tom queried.

"Yep, she's dating the deputy, so I guess she heard something." Clendon said.

"So," Tom began counting on his fingers, "we got a bunch of guys who capture Anderson and feather him up, then," as he touched the second finger,"…we've got Anderson with a bunch of drugs, then two thugs come into town and bust up Woody German," Tom was running out of fingers.

"And someone heard a gun shot over at the Dean's house," Clendon said.

"A gun shot?" Tom asked.

"He said that's what it sounded like, only it was strange because there was a Sheriff's vehicle parked nearby," Clendon said relating what one of his biking buddies had casually mentioned over fries at the Student Union.

"So, I'm saying there's a lot going on we don't know about," said Clendon.

"You know, this is about the last thing we need right now with finals and comps coming up," Tom said shaking his head. If a student wanted to graduate with honors in his department he was obligated to run the gauntlet of oral exams on every subject he had studied for four years in that department and before every professor of the department. It was like opening day of turkey season. You couldn't tell where the next shot would come from.

Tom continued, "I am under a lot of pressure right now to get out the next issue of the paper, and review all this crap from three and four years ago from English teachers who want to be sure I remember what Shakespeare said about this, or what Shelley thought about that."

"Tell me about it. Do you think there is any way we get this closed and over with quickly?"

Tom said, "Not from where I see it today. Maybe something will change."

"In my experience, recently" Clendon said as he rose to go back to his studies, "every time something changes, it just gets worse."

Tom had thought a lot about the current events and what it meant for each side to claim the high ground. "Don't you see the irony in all this?" Tom asked.

"Irony?" questioned Clendon as he lowered himself back in the chair.

"Think about it. You've got one group over here saying the truth is that people have cheated on exams. They say honor means telling the truth about what you've done and perhaps deterring bad conduct by others. As if in confessing one's sins you become honorable."

"Ok," Clendon said.

"Then you've got an opposing group who claims they champion the Honor Code and that honor means in its simplest terms not to lie, cheat or steal, but then resorts to violence to enforce their version of honor."

"I see," Clendon said.

"The irony is that both miss the point," Tom said. "Which of them represents that which is honorable? If you have to pick, which version of honor do you follow? What if in order to act honorably you must injure someone you love or respect?" Tom was racing down paths Clendon hadn't even known were passageways. When Clendon did not immediately respond, Tom continued.

"Is it worse to cheat, and tell the truth about it, or not to cheat and clobber anyone who does? Plato taught that the truth should be honored above men. Listen to this." Tom raised up out of his chair and pulled a book off the shelf above his desk.

He read, "He who intends to be a great man ought to love neither himself nor his own things, but only what is just, whether it happens to be done by himself or by another."

"Plato?" Clendon queried. Not a lucky guess on his part since he could read the book's spine.

"Yeah. I think Plato was saying that we should acknowledge the just and truthful activity of all men as if truth was a fixed constant. Our Honor Code, is in the abstract a very simple concept. It is a way to conduct your own behavior at the highest level," Tom said.

"Similar to the Golden Rule from the Bible?" Clendon asked.

"Not exactly. Say you are an asshole. You treat everyone as an asshole and expect the same from them. That's consistent with the Golden Rule," Tom offered.

Clendon, not about to be outdone by Tom's brilliance and near photographic memory, quoted, "You wear your honor like a suit of armor-you think it keeps you safe, but all it does is weigh you down and make it hard for you to move."

"Nice try, but I've read all *The Game of Thrones*," Tom quickly injected. "So who said,

Honor is the presence of God in man?"

Clendon considered the quote but then admitted, "Don't know."

"Pat Conroy." Clendon and Tom often parried their extensive knowledge of literature into a one on one contest of wits. Late at night and on weekends their group often collected and challenged each other with trivia contests, like "What's the name of Tonto's horse?" One day they would look back on those gatherings in wonder at what glistening young men they had been.

Then Clendon asked, "So, what happens if we never catch the Red Dagger?"

"Maybe we are not supposed to," Tom said. "Perhaps we have met the Red Dagger and it is us."

Sometimes Tom's brain acted with the speed and clarity of light. Clendon nodded and turned to leave still puzzling over Tom's last words.

CHAPTER 31

Ben Ray and Winston Campbell were working out at the gym during a lunch break. Although the weight room would be packed a little later, at the moment there were only a couple of other stringy guys trying like hell to bench 145 pounds. Ben and Winston were not impressed since their normal workout would involve twice that weight.

Ben said, "Just before I left to come over here I heard that the Honor Council has turned up three witnesses who are going to present evidence about," then he said sub voce "Red Dagger at the meeting tonight." Ben looked around to be sure the other two runts had not heard him.

"We isn't that special," said Winston who climbed out of the leg press machine. "Do you know who?"

"Yeah," Ben responded.

"Good. Please ask Darius to visit each of them quickly. That meeting tonight must be over before it begins," Winston commanded as he dropped the 45 pound dumbbells he was doing curls with.

Ben nodded and sprinted out of the weight room, through the front doors of the facility and across campus to the room Darius and his equally huge roommate occupied. Ben's stride was smooth and steady his legs moving with grace like two pistons firing in sync. He was not even winded when he arrived at Darius's room and since the door was cracked he went in pushing it shut behind him.

"Big guy," Ben started.

"What's up Benjamin?" asked Darius who was coming out of the joint bathroom shared with two other students in the adjoining suite. The odor was overwhelmingly foul so Ben begged,

"Can you shut that door big fella, it's hard to breathe in here?" Ben could feel his eyes start to water.

Darius laughed, quite proud of what he had just accomplished in the restroom, "Just a big ol' country dump, my man. Hold on, let me be sure the door to the other suite is open so I can share with the freshmen" He chuckled and pulled the door shut on this side. Ben could finally breathe. It was no wonder Darius could crap like a huge bull with all the food he ate at the training tables. Darius was famous for his "pre-game" dumps before he took the field. It helped everyone out of the locker room faster.

"Three students are going to drop us in the grease at the Discipline and Honor Council meeting tonight. We need to you pay them a special visit and persuade them that would not be the brightest idea they ever had," Ben explained.

"No problem. 'Ol Darius can be very persuasive. Most people don't tell Darius what he don't want to hear," said Darius still chuckling and cracking his knuckles.

Ben pulled his cell phone and hit the send button. Speaking into the phone he said, "We need to locate three students. Yes, the same ones I told you about. Have the guys fan out and call me back on this number as soon as you locate them."

Ben and Darius popped fists and said "boom."

Darius woke up his roommate Cassius and as soon as the calls came back into Ben's phone Darius and Cassius were off on a mission. In a short time Darius would persuade three unsuspecting students that becoming an enemy of the Red Dagger Society was a mistake.

Names and locations were written on a piece of paper Ben handed to Darius. The two big linemen lumbered out the door and down the stairs. As Ben prepared to close the door and leave Darius' dorm room he just shook his head and said "What a pigsty."

The first of the witnesses had just opened his post office box when Darius and Cassius entered the student post office behind him. Cassius blocked the door, and much of the light coming through the glass door so there would be some privacy. The student jumped when Darius came up behind him and placed a bear like paw on his shoulder.

"Yo," said Darius breathing so closely to the

student's face he could smell what Darius ate for dinner last night.

"What?" the student asked nervously. He was a slight fellow and had never been this close to Darius or any other large athlete.

"Little birdie tells ol' Darius you going to talk bad about the Red Dagger Society tonight. That wouldn't be right would it?" Darius' eyes were bulging at rest, now in an animated state he looked scary, like the look he gave opposing lineman who spit tobacco juice on his hand or said something about his momma. For effect Darius had slipped into his south Georgia dialect.

The student stuttered and squeaked out, "I, I, I don't know what you are talking about."

Darius squeezed his shoulder a bit harder, not enough to damage anything but enough to let him know Darius had plenty of reserve power left to go if needed. Darius said, "I think it would be a good idea if you didn't go to that meeting tonight."

The student, now close to a state of shock had begun to sweat. He let out a squeaky little fart and said "I think someone in my family just got sick and I need to run home to check on them."

"That's just what I be thinking," said Darius. "You have a good trip. You don't want Darius paying you a return visit, do you?"

"No, sir," the student said as Cassius stood

aside and permitted him to leave the small mail room.

"Where to now, big boss man?" Cassius asked winking at Darius.

Looking at the sheet Ben had written on Darius said, "looks like we need to go to Foster. Young man there knows something about the truck."

Since Foster was a dorm only a block down from the Post Office, the two giants decided to walk. Burning a few calories only left room for more food at dinner. They located room 105 where witness number two lived. Darius put his hand on the door knob but it was locked. That wasn't a problem since the doors were not solid and the locks were not designed for any real protection. With one twist the door knob and lock broke admitting them into the dark room. The first room contained two desks and a couple of chairs with a floor lamp. Cassius switched on the light near the door and they saw the opening to the bedroom where witness number two was lying in his bed for an afternoon nap. He was only wearing boxer shorts.

"Would you look at that, he's got little Mickey Mouses on his underwear," Cassius said pointing at the prone figure on the bed.

"About the cutest damn thing I ever saw," said Darius who squatted on the single bed opposite the sleeping student. "Hit the lights." Cassius threw the wall switch and a lava lamp came on painting the faintest red glow in the room. Darius liked the effect. Maybe he needed one of these lamps. The student started to wake up and jerked when he saw Darius' dark face in the red light glowing like a tropical voodoo god. As the lamp moved internally the colors flowed across Darius' face and wide brow. He flashed a big toothy grin.

"Hey, buddy, someone told us that you planned on bad mouthing the Red Dagger Society at the hearing tonight," Darius said in an even baritone voice. "We don't think that would be a good idea. I mean for your health and all."

The student clutched at his chest and started hyperventilating. He couldn't speak and Darius could see sweat breaking out on his forehead. A high pitched moan was coming from the student's mouth but Darius just stared back at him. The student still holding his chest glanced up at Cassius who stood like a eunuch in the doorway. His eyes grew wider and he tried to speak,

"I-have-a-heart-condition," he managed to say.

"Well then, don't you think that's a good reason for you not to get messed up in this?" Darius suggested.

Red and crimson washed over the walls and Darius emanating from the now fully charged lava lamp. "Yes, sir," the student said.

Darius pulled his 310 pound frame to full height and said, "Then I think we are on the same page." As he and Cassius walked through the bedroom door into the main part of the dorm room, Cassius said, "Mickey Mouse on his shorts. Jeez."

Their next stop was at the gym. The report they received was that witness number three worked out three days a week at the gym so he should be concluding his exercise program about the time they would arrive. Darius and Cassius strode into the front lobby of the gym nodding at the student proctor at the front desk. As they entered the locker room it was clear there was no one hanging around, but they heard a shower running in the back.

Darius said, "Drop trow Cassius. We are gonna have some fun with this turkey." Darius quickly stepped out of his clothes and moved his glistening naked body toward the shower room. Cassius followed suit. As athletes nakedness did not bother them. Witness number 3 was just turning off the hot steamy shower when Darius and friend walked up buck naked appendages swinging from side to side.

Witness number three looked at the two men trying to keep his eyes off their crotches but he wasn't successful.

"Can I help you?" he asked not sure if he was about to be assaulted or what. Darius, in his most charming and persuasive voice, said, "Come here often? Don't remember seeing you here.

How's the work out going? Building a little muscle mass are we?" Darius reached out and squeezed the student's bicep tenderly. The student was skinny and had the tiniest little bulge of a bicep. It looked like a chicken wing to Darius.

"You look pretty ripped for a white boy," Cassius said, "Don't he Darius?" As he stood there being examined by Darius and Cassius, the student began to get an erection. Oh, my God, he thought. Oh my god, not wanting to look down but knowing what was happening. He quickly backed into the shower and yanked the knob full to the cold side.

Darius leaned on the edge of the shower and said, "Story is you plan on ratting out the Red Dagger Society tonight. I don't think that would be a smart move. Unless you might like me and Cassius here to come back and have a little shower fun which you. You ever played drop the soap with two big beautiful black guys like me and ol' Cassius here?"

The student's eyes were wide and his face and torso were bright pink from the cold water. His former display had shrunk to nothing. He figured he would have to stick his finger up his butt and yell snake to see the little man again. Cassius had begun to flex and stretch like he was a professional body builder. The student's teeth were chattering when he said, "I don't remember nothing."

Darius laughed and said, "Hear that Cassius? This boy don't remember nothing. You better keep remembering nothing. Guess it's time for us to go, my man. That ok with you fella? Best you tell that Committee you got amnesia or something." The student nodded as Darius and Cassius turned and walked back to their clothes laughing all the way. It was amazing how persuasive a little common sense could be.

CHAPTER 32

I had been summoned to the President's Office for a meeting. His offices were in a separate building and were much larger and nicer than what Emily and I shared even combined. I spoke to his Assistant who motioned for me to have a seat. The President's Assistant was tall and a looker in her day. Although she was still a fine looking woman there was a sag here or there signaling the advance of late middle age. A coat rack stood beside the sofa and I took off my overcoat and black Stetson. Following Yogi's advice I had left the logger hat at home. I was not sure the Stetson worked either. Waiting, I looked around at the collection of ancient photographs of the school from the 1800's that covered one wall. On another wall were photographs of men in clerical collars, bishops I assumed. It was as if I had been sent to the principal's office in high school.

The longer I waited the more my anxiety increased. I really needed to get back to my office before the meeting of the committees tonight. I expected to be served a big dose of bullshit by the President but there was nothing I could do to avoid it. There were still a lot of moving pieces to this symphony and I needed to be prepared. After fifteen minutes in purgatory the President's assistant rose and escorted me to the door leading into the President's office. Since she had received no call or instructions while I had been waiting, I suspected she had been told to ice me for precisely fifteen minutes before allowing me entry. She opened the door and stood back allowing me to pass into the chamber. I heard the door close behind me sounding like a vault.

There were three men around a circular table at one corner of the room. I recognized two of them, Bishop Cravens and President Callicott. The third man was tall and seemed familiar but I could not place him. As the President beckoned me over I took long strides extending my hand to the President and then hugged the Bishop in his dark jacket, purple shirt, white collar and gold cross on a chain around his neck. We were way past shaking hands. As I turned to shake hands with the third man he introduced himself.

"Good to meet you Dean Mathews, my name is Winston Campbell, the third," said the man from his six foot four advantage. No wonder he looked familiar since I had met his younger embodiment, Mr. Campbell the fourth on the first night of this adventure.

I nodded and said, "And I believe you are the Chairman of the Board of Trustees?"

He nodded and the President asked us all to sit. My godfather, the Bishop, had a tired sad look in his eyes. The President began, "Jack, this investigation into the so called Red Dagger Society has us all concerned. I have been getting call after call from very influential alumni who are also concerned. Things seem to be spiraling out of control and we cannot let this damage the

University. There is a lot of concern by some very important people." He paused looking straight into my eyes. Remaining quiet I decided to let him have his say.

So, the President continued, "The cost of running this University is only covered fifty per cent by our tuition costs. The rest must come from our endowment and from alumni who have the financial wherewithal to give back generously. I don't need to tell you that a scandal cannot have a positive effect on alumni giving. Just today I received a call from investigative reporters from Chattanooga and Nashville television stations. They are looking into our situation and plan to do some kind of a blasted expose in the next few days. Trailers for this hogwash are already starting to run. It is time we nip this little thing in the bud. It's all been entertaining but it's over." The brows twitched but the glare remained steady.

Mr. Campbell then spoke up, he too holding my eyes in a steely stare, "As the Chairman of the Board of Trustees I am also hearing rumblings among the Trustees who have become aware of this situation. We are in a major fund raising season and cannot tolerate this," his voice booming at the end. Then he continued, "the longer student life is disrupted and the longer there is focus on this situation, the worse it will become for the University. Ultimately, it will fall back on you, and I would hate for you to be the shortest tenured Dean in school history." That laid it all on the table. These guys were threatening me!

My fists were clenching and unclenching but not where they could see. My jaw tightened. I looked over at the Bishop and met his kindly eyes that barely contained a flash of anger. He had seen me like this as a kid when some bully tried to pick on me. What had he drilled into me? Do the right thing and don't worry about the rest? Bullying didn't work then and it wasn't going to work now. I had committed to see this to the end and to do the right thing no matter the consequences. I knew my god father would protect me if he could but it could have slipped out of his control as well. My guts wrenched and I was pissed.

I looked back at the President and the Chairman sucking in a deep breath before I spoke. What I wanted to say was "you sons of bitches" and directly to Campbell "Your own son is up to his neck in this." But, as I exhaled I placed my palms on the table and said directly to my boss,

"Sir, I do not want a scandal or unfavorable publicity any more than either of you. I love this place and I pledged when you hired me to do everything I could to uphold all that is good and dear about this school. *Ecce quam bonum.* Isn't that what it is all about? " I looked alternatively at each of them and went on,

"I think we are in the middle of a crisis, yes, but a manageable crisis and one that falls directly within the jurisdiction of the students themselves. What has gone on here threatens the core of our beliefs. There is no way I can take the consideration of these events away from the duly elected student representatives and maintain any respect in their eyes for the Honor Code or the University. It is one thing to pledge to follow the Honor Code, it is another to live it. I believe that the students will find the correct path and one that does not lead down into the abyss."

The opening stanza to Dante's *Inferno* popped into my head, *Nel mezzo del cammin di nostra vita mi retrovai per una selva oscura che la diritta via era smaritta.* In the middle of the journey of our life I found myself in a dark wood where the straightforward pathway had been lost. I had memorized this once and it had never escaped from my memory. There had to be a way.

I went on, "I also believe the school will be stronger if we let this process work out. If it doesn't you will have my resignation." Come on bully, what's your next move?

The Bishop had a slight smile in one corner of his mouth. He had taught me about resolve and staying true to the mission. Sometimes you had to plunge head long into the rapid without overthinking it. The others continued to look at me as if their x-ray vision would cause me to melt or vaporize any second.

When it was clear I had no more to say and did not intend to surrender, the President said, "I guess we will just have to see won't we? I think this meeting is over."

We all rose and shook hands formally. A firm grip and a nod. I walked out with the Bishop who was holding my arm. His gait was not as steady as it once was, but this time I understood he did not want me to get away just yet.

In the hallway outside the President's office, he pulled me close and said, "I'm proud of you, son. Stick to your guns. You still have friends and those who believe you are on the right path." I gave the old man a hug, nodded and headed back to my office. His support always inspired me to achieve brass rings I might not have the courage to reach for.

CHAPTER 33

Just before 7 pm on Monday night voices buzzed like a disturbed hive as person after person gathered to attend the Executive Committee meeting of the joint Honor Council and Discipline Committee leaders. The Trustees conference room was large with oaked walls and a table that could easily seat twenty people. Along the walls leather chairs were lined up like bishops waiting for the arrival of the Pope. Behind the chairperson's seat was a fireplace and mantle. No fire burned in the structure that was large enough to step into but an antique clock ticked away as the pendulum swung side to side and back making a *click* each time it reached the zenith of its arc. High arched beveled glass windows were cut into the walls along the outer side facing an opposite wall where framed paintings of the founders of the school hung. This bishop and that bishop looked down in judgment at the massive table.

I was sitting to the right of the chairman's seat along the wall beneath one of the windows. Emily came in and touched me on the shoulder whispering "good luck" as she sat down next to me. In other circumstances we would probably have held hands, but not tonight considering the drama that might unfold and how visible our affection would be. On the far wall I saw Jim Wombat with his notepad and recorder among a group of students whom I surmised also wrote for the *Purple Onion*. More students, faculty and even the President with a tall gentleman by his side entered and chose their positions. I did not see Winston Campbell, the third. One group of three chairs was roped off with a sign designating it as reserved for witnesses. These chairs were empty.

At the head of the table sat Clendon Crawford and Ben Ray along with the other Committee officers and the special investigator appointed by each committee. All of the members had been provided legal pads, ink pens and bottles of water. Chatter inside the room pulsed like a wave at a football stadium. Promptly at 7:00 o'clock Clendon called the meeting to order and the room grew quiet as everyone was asked to silence their cell phones. The clock ticked and tocked providing sound effects as if orchestrated by Alfred Hitchcock. It appeared to me that Clendon had assumed control of the meeting and that whatever friction was grinding between him and Ben Ray was not polished smooth yet.

After his welcome Clendon began addressing the members of the Committees, but also for the benefit of the gathered crowd:

"This is a duly called joint meeting of the Executive Committees of the Honor Council and Discipline Committee for the purpose of considering whether or not infractions of the Honor Code or Rules of the University have been violated and whether such actions need to be brought before the full Honor Council and/or Discipline Committee for formal actions. If any of the members have any questions as we move along do not hesitate to interrupt me. Once we begin hearing from the special investigators any member is free to interrupt the speaker with questions concerning the evidence. At the end of the meeting if a majority vote that there is just cause to conduct a full and formal hearing during which penalties may be imposed, we will adjourn and convene full committee hearings depending upon the nature of the charges. Is everyone with me at this point?" Clendon asked. Everyone except Ben Ray nodded. He just looked across the table at Winston Campbell who was seated against the back wall arms folded over his chest.

"Good. Well then, the first item I want to bring up concerns the student, Bob Anderson who wrote a letter to the *Purple* claiming that he had cheated on numerous exams and had observed others doing the same thing. While that would appear to be a clear violation of the Honor Code, because Mr. Anderson is presently at the hospital, we will defer any action concerning him until he is well enough to respond for himself. That leaves us with three other matters to investigate and resolve:

First, the incident regarding a student throwing up into a girl's purse on the last night of party weekend;

Second, the attempted rape or assault of another girl in front of the Sigma Delta house also on the last night of party weekend; and

Finally, the incident of Mr. Anderson's capture

and later return to campus chained in the back of the truck covered with cornflakes and feathers." A muffled giggle went through the room at the image of Anderson decorated like a Thanksgiving turkey.

Emily had her hand resting on my arm as Mr. Crawford continued, "The investigator duly appointed by me as President of the Honor Council is Joan Ward. Ms. Ward would you please begin with your findings?" Well, well. My pretty blonde. Emily had not been pleased when she found the scrap of paper I had accidentally left on the counter in my kitchen. That had sparked a lively conversation between us before I wadded it up and threw it in the trash can.

Ms. Ward was a very tall girl with long blonde hair and green eyes. She was pre-law and intended to become a litigator after law school. There was a natural built in aggression when she spoke and how she moved. Her imposing presence and clear speech had everyone's attention as she fixed her jaw and began with her presentation:

"Thank you Mr. President. I have spent the last several days gathering information about each of the three potential cases. It has not been easy because many students refused to talk or claimed they knew nothing. I have reason to believe witnesses were threatened and one potential witness claims to have developed a medical emergency of his own." There was a collective rush as air escaped from the lungs of several people in the room. Wide eyes looked around nervously. The man next to the President stared right at me.

Ms. Ward continued, " As to the first incident regarding the item in the purse, we have reason to believe this was accurately reported as having occurred between 6:30 and 7:30 pm at the Kappa Zeta house on the last night of party weekend. The female complainant said she had been at several fraternity houses with her date who happened to be a member of the KZ fraternity so they went there last and planned on staying for the balance of the evening. She is certain the object was not in the purse when they left the ATO house but when she went to the ladies room at the KZ house after dancing for about an hour, she opened the purse and found the vomit." Ms. Ward said in disgust.

That's when Ben Ray asked her, "For the record Ms. Ward, can you tell me exactly what was in that purse?" Ray was smiling just slightly as he asked the question deriving pleasure in putting Ms. Ward through this. She was unfazed and replied with surgical precision:

"Mr. Ray, I am sure you know as does everyone on campus. It was P-U-K-E. Puke. Do I need to be any more graphic than that or have I used too large a word for you to comprehend?." She returned his unfriendly fire with optical sights on the bulls eye.

Ray said, glancing around at the group near Mr. Campbell, "No, no. Just wanted to be sure we were dealing with the same purse." More giggles crawled out from the crowd and I could tell some of the guys around Winston Campbell were flushed red trying not to laugh out loud. I was thinking, come on guys and alternately, what a bunch of pricks. Emily's fingers gripped my arm harder and I could tell she was pissed.

Another member of the Honor Council asked, "Do you have any eyewitnesses as to the perpetrator?"

"Yes," Ms. Ward said to a silenced room. "Not only do we have another of the Yearwood girls who saw the purse disappear into the men's room, but she and the victim both positively ID'd the perpetrator from the school directory. We also know that the same student was arrested later that night by the Sheriff's department on public drunkenness charges. I recommend this matter be sent to the full Committee for the appropriate action."

No one was laughing now. I was thinking about Bruce the Purse in the back of Yogi's car that night. Looks like he just got shit-canned. Even cool Winston was squirming now and looked over in my direction. He nodded and mouthed "Let's talk" silently. I nodded back. Things were getting very interesting.

The Executive Committee by a 4-2 vote recommended advancing the tale of the purse to the full Honor Council.

After a short break which Emily and I used to stand up and stretch, I leaned into her ear and said "Come over later?" She nodded and smiled as we waited for Ms. Ward to restart.

When everyone was seated Joan Ward steeled her voice and went on, "In the second case I am afraid we do not have much information. The victim, also from Yearwood, reported that a male jumped on her back and imitated a hunching dog as she tried to get away down the sidewalk in front of the Sigma Delta house. She did not get a good look at her attacker and can make no positive identification. I interviewed five members of the Sigma Delta fraternity who were present at that time but no one saw anything. I am not sure any of them was sober at the time of the occurrence. In this case, I just don't have anything else, unless of course the Discipline Committee has come up with something" she said glancing over at the special investigator of the Discipline Committee, a football player named Darius Jones. Jones just shook his mammoth head and grunted. I didn't expect we would get much help there.

At that point, Clendon Crawford spoke up and said, "Ben that incident falls more within the jurisdiction of the Discipline Committee than anything to do with the Honor Council. What do you want to do?"

Ben Ray said, "Like I said, if there's no proof, there's no proof. We should drop it and move on to something else. That would be my recommendation. How say you?" he asked to the other members of the Discipline Committee. Each of them nodded in unison.

Clendon said, "All right. With nothing more to go on, let's close the hunching incident and move to the abduction of Bob Anderson."

We had come to the main attraction and the crowd sat up. The President had not moved a muscle. Those brows glared stonily in my direction. I leaned into Emily and said, "I am impressed with young Ms. Ward. I think she's a tiger." Emily cocked one eyebrow at me. Oops, I realized too late I had stepped in it again.

The pendulum ticked and tocked back and forth again and again as Ms. Ward carefully reviewed her notes, sipped water and prepared as everyone breathed in short shallow breaths anticipating the drama to come. My eyes continued to sweep the room from the President to the stranger, then to Winston Campbell, and the *Purple* staff. The dynamics swirled like the glisten on the sphere of a soap bubble. I knew this was not a full hearing and that names would not be used, but if the Honor Code was to survive, to have meaning and live in the soul of our school, surely this last matter would have to be handed to the light of day. It would surely need to be fully explored, vetted and those responsible held accountable. I was right wasn't I? The portraits of the Bishops looked down. Would they agree with me or with the money interests? The generals of the various camps were preparing defenses, parries and counter-attacks. I felt the air thick with anticipation and righteousness. Ms. Ward broke the silence.

"Mr. President, and Mr. Chairman," Joan Ward said her eyes moving from Clendon to Ben,"I am very concerned over the status of my investigation into the abduction of Mr. Anderson." Pointing to the chairs marked "Reserved for Witnesses" she said, "You see those chairs. As of this morning I had three witnesses who promised to occupy those chairs at this meeting and tell you what they told me." She turned to the other members at the table and then back at the empty chairs before continuing, her eyes sad with frustration. Her lower jaw jutted out slightly and the muscles in her cheeks flexed. I couldn't take my eyes off her. Unfortunately, Emily had also realized this and elbowed me in the ribs. Ms. Ward went on, "But those chairs are empty. Those chairs are empty because I am convinced those witnesses were threatened, probably by this Red Dagger Society." She almost spit those last words glaring defiantly at Winston Campbell and his crew. Winston met her gaze as a slight smile appeared in one corner of his mouth. Darius Jones had the blank look of a granite statue.

"I have information that the Red Dagger Society fashions itself as a vigilante group of legacy athletes who have pledged to restore honor to this school. Can you believe that?" Ms. Ward projected, her hands flat on the table spread shoulder width in front of her with her head in an attack pose directed strangely at Ben Ray. "Honor?" she asked. "There is nothing honorable about taking another student and subjecting that student to torture and ridicule. They wouldn't know honor if it ran up and bit them on the ass." Tick Tock, Tick Tock. I looked at that damn clock and willed it to shut up. She was working up to a climax.

"Three different witnesses told me they could name members of the Red Dagger Society, one even told me he knew who had driven the truck that brought Anderson back to campus," she stated. "One of those witnesses called me this afternoon and had to go home suddenly for a family illness, another called and recanted everything, and the last one sent me a doctor's order that due to a heart condition he would not be able to testify." Ms. Ward was clearly frustrated that someone had tampered with her witnesses. In itself that would be a violation of the Honor Code. What was going on here? Had the Red Dagger Society won by scaring off witnesses? The thought that students at this school would do such a thing was appalling to me. The stone visaged bishops continued to stare in silence.

As a red-tail hawk from a large roll of hay carefully surveys its domain looking for any sign of movement, I again targeted the persons whom I had begun to hold responsible for this: Mr. Campbell, maybe Mr. Ray, perhaps the other athletes seated nearby. They were no longer holding my gaze.

Ms. Ward went on, "What we do know is

that Mr. Anderson was taken against his will at around 10 pm and not seen again until the following morning. He reappeared chained to the back of a University truck covered with molasses, cornflakes and feathers, wearing a sign that said "I am a cheater". The sign bore the emblem of a knife dripping with blood. " She paused to be certain everyone was fixed on that image.

"Whomever did this to Mr. Anderson are terrorists. This Red Dagger Society apparently claimed credit so I urge the executive committees not to summarily dismiss this investigation. Give me more time to develop witnesses," she pleaded.

Mayhem broke out over the entire room and ricocheted off the oak, glass and stone. Clendon Crawford began rapping his gavel, but I kept an eye on the President and his companion. They were in huddled talk when the tall man suddenly rose, walked to the table and sat at the end facing the committees. He sat there regally in his thousand dollar suit until all was quiet again. Then he began speaking with the finest low country accent.

"My name is Maximillian Burns from Mobile where I practice law with the firm of Burns, Burns and Burns. I am also a graduate of this school and," he paused, "a member of the Red Dagger Society."

My eyes widened and I looked over at Emily who was as puzzled as I. Wombat was writing furiously into his notebook as the girl next to him snapped a photograph of Mr. Maximillian Burns with her cell phone. Where had this come from?

Then he continued, "I appreciate the opportunity to address you. There is much incorrect information going around about the Red Dagger Society and perhaps I can clear up some of the mystery. The Red Dagger Society was actually formed by one of the Bishops hanging on the wall to my right." Burns gestured in the direction of the portraits but did not identify which Bishop.

"The Red Dagger Society is a harmless although secret organization whose simple goal is to preserve those things most dear to this University. Members of the Red Dagger take a lifelong solemn oath to uphold the Honor Code, to protect the identity of its members, and to pass the torch from generation to generation. I am the only member of the Red Dagger you are likely ever to know," he said looking around the table making eye contact with each member. Mr. Burns' gaze communicated that he was a warrior afraid of no one in this room. He had defeated much larger dragons than those presented by the Joint Committees. He went on," members of the Red Dagger have fought in every world war, in Korea, in Vietnam, the Gulf wars, and have served in every branch of our military. Red Dagger members don't hesitate to act when they think the honor of this school has been challenged. I suspect such is the case that Mr. Anderson's letter provided a trigger for the events that followed. Now, some of you may believe that putting molasses, feathers and cornflakes on an admitted cheater is cruel and unusual punishment. Some of you may disagree and may understand why from time to time real men or women must take a stand in the face of evil without regard to personal consequences. One thing has become clear. It was not the Red Dagger Society that caused Mr. Anderson's injuries," he said.

One of the Honor Council officers said, "but, sir, Anderson is in the hospital. How is that not actionable?"

Max Burns replied, "I think you will soon discover that Mr. Anderson was the conductor of his own misfortune. Am I correct Dean Mathews?"

I nodded and rose to address the committees, "That is correct. We have learned Mr. Anderson's blood work contained elements of a dangerous synthetic drug which prompted our email blast that went out earlier today." I was wondering how in the hell this guy knew so much already.

When I sat down, Mr. Burns continued, "So, I am here to tell you that the Red Dagger Society is not your enemy. The event with Mr. Anderson is no different than some of the games played with freshman football players at pre-season camp. You are not likely to discover the identity of any Red Dagger members so I encourage you to close this case and get ready for exams. If you choose not to close the matter, be advised that I am also the lawyer for the Red Dagger Society and we will use every legal resource at our disposal. Litigation, if it comes to that, is full of twists and turns. It is very time consuming and expensive. At the end of the day what will you have accomplished? Nothing. Best not to pick a fight you can't win." With that, Burns rose, thanked the committees, turned his back on the proceedings and left the room. President Callicott rose as well and left.

No one knew what to say. Those collected around the table looked at each other and to me for guidance. I shrugged, it was their meeting. Ben Ray spoke up and said, "I move we close the investigation into the Red Dagger Society."

This prompted Joan Ward to smack her hand on the table and say, "Mr. President, we can't just run from this. Vigilantes do not get to operate above or outside the contract imposed by our Honor Code. I move we do not close this matter." Now all hell was breaking loose again.

Clendon Crawford struggled to restore order and spoke, "The motion on the table is to close the investigation into the Red Dagger Society. All in favor say aye, opposed no." The vote was 3 to 3.

"I guess the motion fails," announced Mr. Crawford. Good for you, Mr. Crawford, I thought. By dealing with Ben Ray's motion first, the fact that it failed meant there was no need to take up the second motion. The investigation was still alive but I was really puzzled. Some of the students wanted action taken, while others did not. As he left the room the President of the University had looked over his shoulder right at me. He understood what had just happened and was not at all pleased. Mr. Burns was certainly an unexpected ringer. I suggested to Mr. Crawford that we would talk tomorrow as he adjourned the meeting.

CHAPTER 34

As Emily and I left the Board Room, Winston Campbell, who had lingered, came over to me and said once again, "We need to talk."

"Ok," I said. "Why don't you meet me at my office first thing tomorrow morning?"

Winston said, "Too late. We need to talk now."

I wondered what couldn't wait twelve hours so I said, "In that case come by my house in an hour." He nodded then pivoted and was gone.

"What was that all about," Emily asked tugging on my arm.

"Not sure, but the mysterious Mr. Campbell needs to meet with me now about something that cannot wait until tomorrow morning," I replied.

"Should I just go on to my house?" Emily asked. Neither of us wanted that option.

"No. We keep our plans the same." I said taking her hand as we left the building. It was a star lit night, cool with the faintest breath of a gentle breeze. The lingering hint of viburnum that scented the air was beginning to fade as the air cooled. Spring was finally coming on. At my house, Rocket bounded past us as she bolted for a pee. Sampson greeted Emily with his usual "mrrow, mrrow" and rubbed up against her legs and feet. For some reason that cat seemed to love Emily's feet more than just about anything.

I lit a small fire and had just poured Emily and me a glass of wine when the knock came at the door. Rocket got there first and growled her low warning growl. I took her collar and let Winston in. He walked into my living room where Emily sat on the sofa with her legs curled up beneath her.

"I'm sorry Dean Mathews. I did not mean to interrupt anything, but I thought we were having a private conversation," Winston said filling the arched opening to the room.

I motioned for him to sit saying, "Ms. Sellars is also an associate Dean. There is nothing you can say that she cannot also hear."

He cleared his throat and began, "I have come into information that I think you and local law enforcement need to be aware of involving Mr. Anderson, along with some of his activities and business associates."

"Okay," I said inviting him to continue.

"In return for this information, I would ask two things of you," Winston said.

"What would that be, Mr. Campbell?" I asked. We eyed each other like fencers waiting for the thrust of the others' blade. Emily had not moved a muscle her glass frozen in space. School officials were not in the habit of negotiating with students. This could establish a bad precedent and I didn't intend to surrender ground to Mr. Winston Campbell, the Fourth.

"Two very simple things: One, have the joint committees drop anything to do with Bruce Sidwell, and two, close the investigation into the Red Dagger Society," he stated and sat back having served to me.

With my arms resting on the side of my chair like President Lincoln at his Memorial I looked straight into Mr. Campbell's eyes and said, "What you ask may not be within my power to grant. What is the information you possess?"

Winston did not go for that ploy. He would continue to negotiate before laying out his information. "Let me state it differently, then. If you believe the information I have to be as critical as I think you will find it to be, will you do *everything* in your power to grant the two conditions?" he asked.

I nodded and looked over at Emily who had moved her wine glass to her lips and sipped clearly enthralled with our negotiations. "If you have valuable information Mr. Campbell that works to the benefit of this school why don't you simply provide it to me? For the good of the school, of course," I said.

"I guess I could simply inform law enforcement, but there is some question concerning the identity of all who are involved. I am not sure whom I can trust," he said. "I can't explain certain things unless there is some connection to the local Sheriff's department."

This was the same feeling I had considered when the Mexicans borrowed Anderson's computer from this very room a few days earlier. Only Yogi knew I had it. I said, "Then I think we have an understanding. I give you my word."

Emily asked Winston if he would like anything to drink and went into the kitchen barefooted to get him a glass of ice water. He watched her backside as she stepped into the kitchen. When she was gone he blushed and turned back to me. I said, "Don't get any ideas, big boy." He nodded and when Emily returned with his glass, he began,

"I have learned that Mr. Anderson's roommate was a major supplier of drugs, mainly pills and dope, for a Mexican drug ring."

"Not Anderson, but his roommate?" I asked.

Winston continued, "What you don't know is that when Bruce Sidwell was taken to the county jail by Deputy Baker, he was visited by a Mexican who has recruited him to replace the roommate." Now that was something new. Bruce the Purse as the new drug runner?

"You see why I am not sure who can be trusted," Winston said.

"I share some of that same concern," I

admitted.

Winston now thinking of us as allies, said, "Tomorrow night at 9 pm Bruce is to meet with the Mexican agents to close the deal and become the next runner. That meeting is to take place at the Forestry Cabin. Bruce came to me because he does not want to be any part of this. He is really scared but will do whatever to help put an end to this. I know law enforcement should be involved but I am not sure what to do. I have also been advised to get Deputy Yogi Baker in the loop."

"Let me talk to him," I said. "You have done the right thing. This information will be most helpful. I would appreciate it if you and Mr. Sidwell would come to my office first thing in the morning. Don't say anything to anyone else. If either of you miss a class, I will write a permission slip." Winston rose and with a glance at Emily that lasted just a bit too long for my liking left my house.

After the door closed, Emily asked, "Now what?" I had mixed feelings about granting amnesty to the Red Dagger but the ability to work with law enforcement to put an end to the Mexican threat meant everything right now. I hoped my deal with the devil wouldn't backfire.

"Now Yogi and I need to clear the air, and I need to call Special Agent Bradley, " I said picking up my cell phone and speed dialing Bradley. He had returned to Nashville but said he could be back on the mountain tomorrow morning. Unfortunately, his ability to bring reinforcements on such short notice was limited. Bradley mentioned he would bring "Arnold" with him.

My next call was to Yogi who was out on patrol near the interstate. He could be to my house within twenty minutes. My gut told me I could trust Yogi. I had to, he was my best friend and confidant. My inclination was to take Emily home but I knew that she was dug in and intended to be part of the unfolding resolution. If I tried to exclude her now "because she was a girl" it could do irreparable damage to our relationship, and I couldn't let that happen. Twenty minutes later the patrol car pulled up outside. Somehow Rocket knew it was Yogi and was doing her full body wiggle waggle when he knocked.

Yogi was in full uniform weapons belt and all. He came on in the living room said hello to Emily and declined a beer since he was still on duty.

I had decided to level with Yogi. I had taken his measure as a man and a friend for many years and he had never failed me. He had never failed to do the right thing. So, I began, "Yogi, we thought that Bob Anderson, the student who was tar and feathered was a drug dealer for a group of Mexicans. Now it seems it was his roommate who withdrew from school. Those same Mexicans are recruiting another of my students. They recruited him, Yogi, while he was in your jail."

Yogi was stunned. "In my jail? How is that?" he asked defensively. His reaction to the news had been genuine. He knew nothing about the encounter between Bruce and the Mexican.

"I don't have the particulars but the second day he was there one of these Mexicans came into his cell and began the recruitment," I said watching for Yogi's reaction. Again, I saw no evidence he was lying to me.

"That was the day I was sent with the drugs we found over to Nashville with Bradley," Yogi said scratching his head. "Jack, when you told me the Mexicans came to your house and took the computer, I got real worried because except for you and me, the only person who would have known the whereabouts of that computer was someone who read my report. That means there could be four or five others in my own department involved." Yogi then told us he had been concerned for several months that something was wrong in the department. Little things like a piece of evidence disappearing or the wrong amount of cash turning up after a bust had begun to worry him. Then this Anderson thing happened and his Uncle was paying close attention to the whole investigation with much more attention than he had shown lately about anything else the department was working on.

"That's why it's up to us to put an end to this now. Bruce Sidwell is cooperating with us and we need to formulate a plan of action for tomorrow night. I have spoken with Bradley who will be here in the morning with a guy named Arnold," I said.

Yogi laughed, "Arnold is something special, but he's not a guy."

That's when Emily said, "Then what is he, some kind of friggin' pig?"

"Nope. You'll see. Jack, I'll be at your shop early," Yogi said as he left.

Emily and I talked late into the night about the Joint Committee meeting, the Honor Code, and about us as the fire burned low. A sleep over seemed like a good idea.

CHAPTER 35

At the end of a cul de sac in Northwoods at the edge of the city's street lamps, a police cruiser idled while a large SUV pulled up next to it. One man exited the SUV and opened the door climbing into the cruiser. He turned to the man in uniform sitting with his hands on the steering wheel and said,

"Is everything set for tomorrow night?"

The officer scratched the side of his head and looked back. "Yes, Elias, I think so," he said. "I have made sure no one will be using the Forestry Cabin so it will be available to us. It is very remote and private. There will be no prying eyes. Only one road leads into the cabin."

"Good," the Mexican nodded.

"And how about your end?" the officer asked. "Will the young man show up?"

Elias responded, "He has five thousand reasons to show up."

"But, what if he doesn't show up?" questioned the officer.

"Then," Elias said, "we work on another plan after we deal with Mr. Bruce. Why do you ask so many questions, my friend?"

The officer knew he was in over his head and wanted out. There just didn't seem to be any good solution that would let him out of the web he had fallen in. Now, he had begun to sample a bit of the product himself and his marriage was going to shit at the same time. What he wanted was to run as far away as he could, far away from Elias, the sheriff's department, and all of it. The spidery eyes of the Mexican studied his face.

"Just trying to be sure we have covered all the bases," he said after a moment fighting to keep the tension out of his voice.

"My men and I will meet you at the place tomorrow evening. Nothing should go wrong, Senor, or our benefactor will not be happy," Elias said as he stepped out of the police vehicle. The officer watched the SUV pull away and put his forehead against the top of the steering wheel. How had it all gone so bad?

CHAPTER 36

Early the next morning, while the rest of the campus was only beginning to rise, my office was already humming with activity as Yogi, Bradley, Winston Campbell, Bruce Sidwell, Leon Allgood, Emily and I huddled over a topographical map of the mountain Leon had brought from the maintenance office. Leon was invited because he knew the mountain better than anyone. Once, Leon had showed me how to locate old Indian trails in the woods at night not by looking down but by looking up and following the open path presented as the tree branches parted on account of a footpath. In low light conditions this was a much more reliable guide. I trusted his skills in the woods. Leon told me on one such trip that he was part Cherokee, as was Yogi, I thought.

"Show me the Forestry Cabin, Mr. Allgood," Bradley instructed. The big man pulled the map over to him, and said,

"It's Leon" as his large square finger traced the gravel road out to the cabin resting on top the symbol for the cabin. Bradley put a red "X" on the symbol.

"Looks like only one way in and one way out," Yogi said also following the black dashes representing the road. The cabin sat about five miles from campus out the old road leading beside the farm where Rocket and I had been running a few days ago. In a clearing in the middle of a pine stand the cabin had been constructed and maintained by the Forestry Department as a primitive research station. It was a rustic all wood structure and could be reserved for special events.

"Tell me about the cabin itself," said Bradley.

"One way in and one way out," said Winston. "It's a log structure about 20 by 20, two windows on the door side and a fire place at the other end. Big porch across the front. Usually there are some wooden straight back chairs and a picnic table near the fireplace. There's no back door." I glanced over at Emily whose return look communicated she also thought Winston sure knew a lot about that cabin for a political science major.

"If there's only one road leading out there, how to we gain any element of surprise?" asked Emily. The others in the room weren't aware she was part of the assault squad and I could see glances being exchanged.

Leon spoke up, "See this?" He was pointing at a faint dashed line maybe 200 yards off in the woods to the west of the cabin. We all followed his finger as it traced all the way back to within 50 feet of the University maintenance shed where Leon worked a few miles distant.

He went on, "That's an old logging road that hasn't been much used since those woods were cut almost twenty years ago. It is possible in sturdy four wheel drive trucks to get very close to the cabin."

Leaning over the map, I followed the logging road towards the cabin and saw very tight contour lines from the road up to the clearing. "Leon," I said, "if I am reading this map correctly, those tight lines mean a steep grade from the logging road up to the cabin. Right?"

"Yeah, the tighter the lines the steeper the grade, but it's doable. There is a cut line from here to here that connects to another trail terminating at the cabin itself," Leon said. Everyone continued to study the map as a plan was forming.

Bradley asked, "Mr. Sidwell, what are your instructions?"

In a shaky voice, Bruce said, "I am to ride my motorcycle to the cabin at exactly 9pm. The Mexicans said they would be waiting in the cabin with my first delivery and cash up front. Then they will tell me how to decode the email I will receive from the intermediary."

"Intermediary?" asked Yogi.

"Yes. Some guy who is to be my local contact," Bruce said.

"So," Bradley said, "we can expect there will be at least four people in the cabin when you arrive. We can also anticipate they will be armed." That last statement caused me to catch my breath. It should have been obvious but I had not focused on that aspect of our plan.

"I don't have much appetite for putting any students, or me or Emily in a line of fire," I said defensively.

"You won't be with me and Yogi, and Arnold there," said Bradley, "Assuming everything goes as planned. On the safe side do you have any guns, just in case, you know?"

"I've got a 12 gauge semi with the plug out that can hold five shells," I said.

"Okay," Bradley replied, "load it with buckshot, none of that wimpy 7.5 target load. What about the rest of you?"

"I've got a 9mm Beretta," Emily responded to my amazement. I looked over at her my eyebrows cocked.

"Bring it."

Leon said, "I've got lots of guns." I was not surprised since Tammy had told me he had been in the Army and he was, well, local.

"Me too," said Winston. Great, I thought. If this got screwed up and people started shooting, I was fucked big time.

"Mr. Campbell, I need about four strong guys to help me get Arnold up the hill," Bradley said as he pointed at the topo map.

"That will not be a problem," Winston promised.

"Get Arnold up the hill? Where is he" I asked.

"Oh, he's out in the truck," Bradley said. Now, I was really confused. There was some secret Bradley and Yogi shared but so far not with the rest of us.

"Arnold is a special, special agent of the TBI," Bradley announced. I was waiting so Bradley continued with a grin on his face, "Arnold is the latest version of the Robotex Avatar robot equipped with a Safariland Tri-Chamber canister. That canister is full of a chemical agent commonly known as tear gas. He is also radio controlled and with cameras so we can see what is happening from a safe distance." I could tell Bradley was really into all this high tech police work. He probably had a Dick Tracy decoder ring as a kid.

"No shit?" said Winston.

"Yep, Arnold has many redundant capabilities. His extension arm can be equipped with a .40 caliber machine pistol. He can go over and around almost anything. The only drawback here for us is that he weighs around 100 pounds outfitted and I don't want to risk bringing him up that hill on his own power," Bradley explained. "That's where your guys come in." Bradley pointed at Winston who nodded.

Bradley continued, "Bruce, I won't sugar coat this, but you will be inside with the Mexicans when Arnold ignites the gas. Here is a pair of protective goggles. Slip them in your jacket pocket and when Arnold unleashes hell , drop and roll and put these on. You will still get gassed unless you can hold your breath for a long time. But, I want you down and out of the way. Once we have neutralized the bad guys we will come in and get you. I would get you a full gas mask but it's too bulky and we can't hide it on you well enough. You must remember that you will be going into the cabin last. Do not latch the door. That's important because that's how Arnold will go in."

Bruce nodded and took the goggles, but his shaking hands betrayed his fear. Winston put his hand on his shoulder and whispered something in his ear.

"I want us to be in position well in advance of the meeting. Leon, we will meet at the maintenance shop at seven. You will lead with your truck. I will follow with Arnold in mine. Any questions?" Bradley was in charge now. He had a plan, and it seemed sound to me. I didn't know what else we could do and this had to end. I hoped we could trust everyone on our team.

CHAPTER 37

It was the longest day of my life full of indecision and doubt. I went over our plans looking for mistakes time and again to the point that I could not deal with anything else. Routine meetings and calls were dreamlike and I had no interest and no focus. Emily came in several times and just sat opposite my desk. Looking at her I could tell the same things bugging her were likewise bugging me. What were we missing? What detail have we overlooked, and how in God's name could we send Bruce Sidwell into that cabin?

Everything seemed to be happening out of sync either too fast or in slow motion. With time tangled in a sticky web there were too many alternatives and what ifs. In the abstract I felt we were doing the right thing yet I still feared we could not stop the drug supply by arresting three underlings. Were we just going to make things worse? My students could be injured or killed. The one thing that kept advancing the day was the idea that this was our only opportunity and if we hesitated we might not have the chance again.

Part of me was exhilarated with the thrill of the hunt like walking a field of cane with a good dog anticipating the flush of a pheasant. However, the saner me, the little guy on my shoulder, kept saying "take a deep breath" and "stay out of it" or "have you lost your fucking mind?" I finally decided we were in it up to our eyeballs, one way or another. This would be resolved tonight.

Emily and I grabbed a sandwich and sat under a tree in the Quad talking low so we would not be overheard. The occasional student passed by on the way to a class and nodded to one or both of us.

She said, "Assuming no one is hurt, which may be a huge assumption, if this doesn't work out we are both likely to get fired."

"Yeah," I said acknowledging the truth of her statement. "I wish you would stay home tonight."

Emily jerked up and looked at me hard. "No way. We're both in this together. Besides if it comes to it, you haven't seen me shoot yet."

Christ. Shooting? Really? Was there a reckless side to her I was just seeing? I shook my head and said, "There can't be any shooting, Emily. None, do you hear me?"

"Wouldn't you shoot if it meant protecting someone?" she asked.

"Only as a last resort," I responded.

"You can't hesitate in such a situation, Jack. Hesitation can mean getting hurt."

I knew she was probably right but when had she turned into Annie Oakley on me? I asked, "Where did you get these instincts about shooting and all?"

We had not talked much about our lives between college and returning to the University. There had probably been relationships for both of during that decade. It was a sensitive area we were not ready to explore. Emily looked up from her food and said, "Let's say I had some formal training."

"Formal training?" I repeated.

"There was a time when I was at Quantico," she said.

"You were military?" I asked caught completely off guard.

"FBI," Emily said.

"FBI?" I was now sounding like a parrot. "What happened?"

"Someone got hurt. I don't want to talk about that right now, okay?" Emily said closing up her brown paper sack that held the remnants of her lunch. This conversation had killed her appetite. We went back to our offices to deal with whatever routine matters could be handled without much effort or emotional attachment. My mind raced around the idea of Emily as FBI. Who had gotten hurt, and why? There were a lot of questions I had for her but it would have to wait. I had to concentrate on this evening's plan.

Emily and I left the office about 5pm and went to my house where we adopted the dark clothing everyone had agreed upon, nibbled at a little food, and tried to relax before the storm. Rocket was tense and must have known something unusual was approaching like the way the air changes pressure and smells of ozone before a big clap of thunder splits the sky. I handled Emily's "9" and told her I would not have thought she would have owned such a weapon. She told me she had dated a Navy Seal once who taught her how to shoot. Interesting. FBI and a Seal? I knew I would have to leave those topics to another day. There was still a lot we had to learn about each other.

We climbed into my Jeep arriving at the maintenance shed as the sunset was giving way to a cloud bank rising in the western horizon. There would be no moon tonight. Special Agent Bradley checked everyone's clothing, weaponry and went through the plan a final time. Winston Campbell introduced two very large football players, Darius Jones and Cassius Turner, who in dark clothing almost disappeared as it grew darker. Looking at these huge guys all I could think was I sure wanted them on my side. Yogi got in the TBI vehicle with Bradley. Two of the players climbed in the back with Arnold, while the rest of us piled into Leon's Dodge Powerwagon.

The old logging road had begun life as a mule trail before modern equipment permitted trucks to cut and load timber. The twin tracks were deeply rutted making our travel an up and down bump followed by a lurch where we bottomed out again. Leon coaxed the big Dodge along through the forest avoiding what he could and working not to throw anyone out the back. At times we had to move closer to the center of the bed to avoid being scraped off by the overgrown and overhanging limbs. I was hoping I could still walk after bouncing up and down on my tailbone. After we had bounced along for about half an hour, Leon cut the headlights and slowed to a stop. I guessed we had arrived.

We gathered in a huddle around Rockie Bradley who said in a soft voice, "OK guys. We have got one hour to get up this hill and into position. No flashlights and minimum talking." He looked around at everyone and continued,

"The connector trail is about ten yards over there." Bradley pulled out a red beam flashlight and pointed. "You big guys are with me. We are going to the tree stand across from the door. Dean, you, Leon, and the lady stay to my left on the west side of the cabin. The road comes in from the right side and that's how our friends will arrive. Yogi, once the Mexicans have cleared their car you take up a position by their vehicle. Do not let anyone try to escape in their vehicle."

Yogi nodded. Carefully, as if they were moving a crate of nitro, the football players lifted the tarp off and helped Bradley pull Arnold to the end of the truck bed where Bradley attached two bars on either side to be used as hand grips. Arnold stood there about 36 inches high his polished surfaces glowing red from Bradley's light. Standing ready for battle, Arnold looked invincible and magnificent. He was not quite the Terminator but pretty intimidating anyway. On either side of his central unit ran a metal track with gripping treads. These tracks reminded me of a Bradley tank only smaller. On one side an arm extension was fitted with the Safariland canister. For balance the arm on the other side was connected to a mechanical hand with a wide metal plate where fingers would have been and an opposing thumb. Up and out the tailgate Arnold was lifted and began the climb up the path in the iron grips of Darius, Cassius, Winston and Ben Ray. The students started moving as a single unit advancing Arnold to his target. No one spoke. Near the end of the path I could just make out the cabin's roof silhouetted against the sky. No light came from the cabin but there was enough afterglow from the sunset to distinguish trees and bush from stalking humans.

Bradley motioned with his left hand for Leon, Emily and me to peel off and take up our positions on the left. The rest stayed in the cover of the woods moving slowly to the right. From what we could see there were no vehicles anywhere in sight. Once Bradley was lined up opposite the door the players sat Arnold down and the bars were removed. A path was cleared so Arnold would have a direct shot to the front of the cabin. Silently, the boys gathered pine limbs and camouflaged Arnold so he became invisible. Yogi moved to the right flank.

Emily and I were on one knee behind a pile

of fallen trees with Leon between us and Bradley's position. Although we were armed, the plan only called for Emily and me to act if all else failed. The balance of our team was either law enforcement, ex-military or, I thought, Red Dagger? It was oddly quiet interrupted only by the cry of a sentinel whippoorwill expressing his love for a missing mate. We were breathing slowly to settle our nerves when we began see the headlights from two vehicles slowly coming down the road from way off. The beams bounced off trees and canopy until the vehicles arrived in the gravel area near the cabin and cut the lights. For a couple of minutes nothing moved, then three men got out of the suburban and one man exited the Sequoyah County Sheriff's vehicle. We couldn't make out faces but the three who left the suburban were about the right size for the guys who had taken Anderson's computer. Something was said and for a moment the figure who had exited the Sheriff's vehicle turned as if he was going back to his car. We watched as one of the others hurried over to him and grabbed his arm. More words were exchanged and the officer was shoved in the back toward the door of the cabin.

The four men entered the house and latched the door. A light began to glow orange from the inside as a lantern was lit. One of the men had been carrying a bag. I looked down at my shotgun and pushed the safety forward exposing the red active dot. I had already confirmed there was a shell in the chamber full of buckshot that would cut a man in half at close range. At the same time I heard Emily rack a round into her pistol. Both

Emily and I were locked and loaded but our palms were sweaty despite the coolness of the night. I saw Emily wipe her palm on her jeans and I did the same.

Soft murmurs of conversation came from inside the cabin. I looked over at Emily as she intensely focused on the cabin. It seemed to me she was liking this hunt a little too much. Had I missed something about her? Was it something to do with that damn Seal?

A single light came down the road as Bruce's BMW motorcycle pulled into the area beside the SUV. Bruce set his bike and looked around. Bradley had told him that it was important to get him inside the cabin with his cell phone set to record and for the transaction to occur before we acted. He had told Bruce earlier to expect action about five to seven minutes after he went in and be sure not to latch the door. Bradley emphasized not latching the door over and over.

I realized my mouth had gone dry. I had been hunting before, but never where my prey had the ability to shoot back. I was ok with being on the periphery of the action. Yogi would remain cool under fire, and I hoped Bradley was not all hat and no horse when things got tight.

Like a ghost I saw one of the students move closer to Arnold and begin removing his pine bough cover. A small red light came on as SA Bradley fired up Arnold and tested his remote controls. The robot's camera was active but not emitting any light that might reveal his presence. High powered halogen lights were installed along the front but were not active. Standing stationary there was no sound coming from Arnold, but I was concerned once he started moving it might be a different story. Sound would be our enemy. At a minimum he would likely crunch gravel as he cleared the parking lot. Surely, the gears would spin and engage as he climbed the steps, and that would alert our targets inside the cabin, wouldn't it?

We had considered using someone other than Bruce to go into the cabin for this meeting but realized at least one and maybe more of the Mexicans had seen Bruce up close already. If someone other than Bruce walked in that door they would know their plans had been blown and react accordingly. That eliminated any stand-in. Bravely, Bruce strode up to the door and entered without hesitation. Don't latch the door. Don't latch the door, I was willing Bruce's mind from my hideout. A second later Emily and I heard the metallic sound of the door latch behind him and Emily exclaimed "Oh shit. I don't think Bradley heard that."

I could see Yogi in the shadows moving along the tree line then crossing behind the SUV and kneeling along the side of the bulky vehicle. Emily and I were actually closer to the door than Bradley and I didn't think Bradley could have heard the latch either from where he was. Under orders not to move or risk disclosing our presence we had even left all cell phones in the trucks. I couldn't warn Bradley that the door had latched.

Holding the remote control console to his gut and working the controls with his right hand, Bradley slowly engaged Arnold as his twin tank like treads on either side of the chassis sprang to life. Silently, Arnold was advancing in the dark to the steps leading up to the front porch of the cabin. I was amazed that he, or it, moved so silently. I would have expected whirring or some mechanical sound, but Arnold was built for stealth. The rubber treads and their spaced configuration also muffled the noise of the pea gravel over which he was moving toward the first of the steps.

Emily whispered, "How is it going to get up the steps?"

"Bradley said steps were no problem for Arnold," I whispered back. We continued to watch as Arnold moved silently across the gravel to the edge of the first step. Then our little soldier started up each step, its treads engaging and grabbing for enough purchase to move steadily up onto the porch. I knew the moment had come when the plan either succeeded or failed. Each time the little soldier gained a step it teetered up and back slightly as if a breath could topple it backward and crashing down the steps. But with each step a tread found traction and righted him. Two steps, three steps, then Arnold gained the edge of the porch.

Bradley moved Arnold into position directly in

front of the door then turned him to the left moving to the edge of the window. Arnold's left arm, the one with the mechanical hand, also had a camera mounted on the back of the wrist joint. Carefully Bradley raised the arm until the camera could look into room without being detected. He hit "record" and ran the video for sixty seconds. I did not know if the electronics were sensitive enough to pick up sounds within the cabin. The arm retracted to the robot's side. Bradley moved Arnold back into position at the edge of the porch in front of the door and pushed the forward lever down hard. Arnold went charging into the door with a loud thump but the door didn't budge. Emily had guessed correctly that Bradley did not hear the latch click behind Bruce.

The thump had not gone undetected inside either. Now we began to hear voices inside and the scraping of chairs against the wood floor. As our plan began to crumble like too dry cornbread, Bradley stood and furiously guided Arnold back and to the side in front of the window. In one movement Arnold's extension arm fitted with the canister raised four feet into the air and Arnold charged the side of the cabin. The arm shattered the glass of the window and Bradley ignited the canister. That's when all hell broke loose.

As soon as the canister flashed we were moving with guns drawn toward the cabin as it filled with tear gas. Everything was chaos. Now I could smell the gas too. People inside and outside the cabin were yelling and coughing. It was obvious the men inside the cabin could not remain there. They had to come out and face whatever threat was on the outside. We knew these were men of action and although blinded by the gas and disoriented would still be dangerous. We had practiced how we would react when they finally came out, but in real life it was different. You could not predict with any degree of accuracy what the men would do.

The door was flung open and Mexicans began to stumble out. It was not a charge as we had feared but more of a loose stumble. The first man was met by Darius who had jumped from the ground to the porch in one leap. I was amazed a big guy could do that. Darius grabbed the man's jacket and flung him off the porch like tossing a bale of hay. Cassius was waiting. The gun flew out of the Mexican's hand as he landed with a thud. That's when Cassius reached down snatching him up and put the little man in a bear hug with his arms pinned to either side. The little Mexican squirmed and yelled but he was still unable to see Cassius who squeezed harder and harder until the man passed out. Cassius dropped him to the ground like a sack of potatoes and applied cuffs Yogi had brought along.

As the next Mexican lunged out and reached the porch he couldn't see Arnold behind him and ready for combat. With one move Bradley had Arnold's throttle pressed full forward as the mechanical hand reached out and grabbed the second Mexican right in the cheek of his ass tightening as he pushed the Mexican off the porch dragging Arnold with him. He too lost his weapon and crashed onto his face in the pea gravel with Arnold on top of him. Bradley activated the speaker built into Arnold's mainframe and Arnold ordered his prisoner, "stop all resistance, you are under arrest" in a mechanical voice that sounded somewhat like the Governator. Arnold's steel hand had a good chunk of the Mexican's ass cheek and was not letting go. It was only seconds before Bradley had him cuffed as well but Bradley was not finished with this greaser just yet.

Something rushed over me and without hesitation as the third Mexican appeared I bounded up the steps and crashed the gun stock of my Benelli into his teeth saying, "That's for my dog." The man went down hard face first into the gravel at the base of the steps. Emily cuffed him like roping a young calf and I pulled him to the side. "Nice move, cowboy," she said.

"You too," I yelled.

We still had our weapons trained on the door when the fourth man came out his service pistol drawn but too gassed to see clearly. He had been breathing the tear gas longer than any of the others. As he shuffled toward the steps Yogi kicked him in the side of the knee which immediately collapsed. He yelled tumbling down the steps. The fourth man looked up into Yogi's .357 revolver aimed at his temple when he rolled over.

"Shit," Yogi said, "Hello, Uncle Buford." Clearly shaken, Yogi stepped on the man's wrist and twisted away his firearm. No shots had been fired. The second Mexican was screaming as Arnold began dragging him by the ass across the gravel. Once again Bradley was having a big time with technology playing with Arnold's controls. We got Bruce out safely although the tear gas had filled his lungs. With the help of Winston, Darius and Cassius we collected the weapons and secured each of the Mexicans and Sheriff Baker into the back seat of either the patrol car or the suburban. Yogi left in the patrol car with the Sheriff headed back to the Northwoods station. I followed in the suburban with Emily riding shotgun her 9mm aimed at the back seat and our Mexican guests. Their eyes grew large as Emily's eyes narrowed.

"Just do something stupid," she said to the prisoners. The three sat there defeated, heads down. A couple of them continued to spit blood all over the floor and back seat. It was okay, not my car. They weren't going to try anything. They could tell this lady was the real deal. So could I.

Leon and Bradley went back to their trucks. The four students grabbed Arnold and carried him back down the logging road and into Bradley's truck. As I pulled away I heard the men carrying Arnold singing some rowdy bar song. The tension that had oppressed us had vanished with the realization the plan had worked.

CHAPTER 38

Two months later I was sitting just below the spillway on the Ocoee River at the river right put in used for open canoes performing the same pre-run ritual I did each time before I paddled this river. Sitting in about 18 inches of water I let the water flow over my feet and legs while I splashed more on my chest and face. My mind chanted "One with the river", "one with the river". At some point in my training as a whitewater paddler I had come to believe the river gods would let me pass safely if I did this, because, you see, this river will kill you. The sheer volume and force of the current as it erupts down the spillway can take a canoe or kayak and dash it against granite boulders or suck it into bottomless holes if the river gods are angry. My hope was that the religious ceremony showed my respect for this river and those gods. In return I would be granted dispensation to navigate the river safely.

This put in was just below the first rapid known as Grumpy's and gave us a microsecond to adjust to the push of the river before entering the maw of the rapids. If the power company is generating power all the force of the river is directed into a wooden flume that parallels the left side of the river high along the bluff until it crashes down metal tubes into the turbines at the Powerhouse. Today, they were not generating power and the force of the river was on display in front of us.

Yogi and I had decided to make the run from Dam #2 to the Powerhouse and down to the new take out parking area as we had done on many prior warm days in Polk County, Tennessee. This river had been home to the Olympic whitewater course for the Atlanta Games. The river upstream from where we were had been reconstructed into a narrow course of boulders and rapids. Once I was strapped in, I peeled out into the current in my OutrageX open canoe feeling the current catch and turn the bow as my Silver Creek paddle stuck a pivot point and I was off. Yogi followed in his Whitesell. Together we slipped into the current navigating over drops and through chutes catching eddies and bailing as necessary. At Moonshoot we lined up river right and flew between rocks with barely enough room to stick a paddle in the water. Then it was eddy left and eddy right as we played above the approach to Broken Nose.

After a few trips as a paddler you learn that the naming of rapids is an art form and is usually descriptive of what is getting ready to happen or what has happened to some sucker in the past, in case your sight line is obstructed and you are in the middle of the action before you can read the water and pick out the best route. The absolute worst thing is to have a rapid named after you because it means you probably did something really stupid right at that spot. Broken Nose was like that with the force of the water shoving to the right over a couple of ledges and into sucking holes. The fact that the rapid was not described as "Bob's Broken Nose" but simply generically probably meant more than one paddler had bit the dust at this spot.

The thing about the Ocoee as it runs along Tennessee Highway 74/68 is the sense of accomplishment when you get through the last rapid at Powerhouse and float to the take out. Navigating the river is a rush but completing the journey is special. You realize you are still alive and the river gods were appeased. For hours you have been concentrating on each line through each rapid, individually named and always different from the last one with countless strokes and pivots. There is no time to think about anything else, unless you want to swim a rapid separated from your boat, which I do not recommend having done that on more than one occasion. The act of concentrating on staying alive and out of the way of rafts has the effect of pushing all other cares and troubles to the back.

Below Table Saw rapid Yogi and I caught the big pool eddy on river left and got out of our boats to stretch and eat lunch. Cheese, crackers and Vienna sausages tasted like the finest filet mignon as raft after raft of screaming tourists shot by and into Witches' Hole.

Yogi asked, "has everything been resolved at the school now that the semester is over?"

"Pretty much," I said taking a long drag off my diet Dr. Pepper and burping." I still have a job. You know the story on Anderson. When he was well enough to leave the hospital he was cleared on the drug charges. The computer actually belonged to the missing roommate. Still, I don't know Anderson is coming back. Poor guy didn't deserve that torture."

"I bet he wishes he had never written that stupid letter to the *Purple Onion,*" Yogi mused.

"Or gotten the Red Dagger pissed off," I added. "We didn't hear much out of any of the gypsies for the rest of the semester either. Henry Chen, Winston Campbell and Ben Ray all graduated on time, Henry and Winston with honors," I said as I flicked a piece of cracker into the water and watched a minnow jump at it.

"Fish are finally beginning to come back to this water after the mess all the copper mining created upstream back in the thirties," I said.

Yogi said, "I hear the fishing is pretty good when they are generating power and the flume is in operation." When water runs in the flume the river gets very shallow and the current is routed down miles of wooden flume and then into the turbines at Powerhouse.

"May be," I grunted "but would you really eat anything that came out of this river?" I knew that if you even got a cut or scratch from this river it took forever to heal. Six months and the sore wouldn't heal.

"Not likely," Yogi chuckled.

I continued, "I kept my agreement with Mr. Campbell and at my suggestion both the Honor Council and the Discipline Committee terminated their investigations on account of a lack of evidence. Several of the students were disappointed with that outcome, but I think we talked it out. The ones going into finals and comps were actually relieved."

"Both the Red Dagger and the purse deal?" Yogi asked with a little too much emphasis on the Red Dagger part.

"Do you know something I don't Yogi?" I asked.

"Nope, just asking," Yogi said as I watched him stare into the river. I was sure he was holding something back on me, something bigger than our friendship. Something bigger than this river.

So, I went on, "The President was happy, that lawyer Burns was happy. Everybody was happy, happy, happy. Except, Miss Ward who wanted to nail the Red Dagger. That girl seems to be obsessive about things. She hasn't given it up and I understand is planning to petition the Board of Trustees. She seemed shocked when I told her "good luck with that" and explained who the Chairman of the Board of Trustees was. She will learn. After those guys helped put away the dealers, I just didn't see anything else I could do considering my agreement with Mr. Campbell. That Sidwell kid had some real nuts to go in that cabin. Perhaps the

Red Dagger was our friend all along and maybe I can rationalize their version of honor." More rafts of screamers lunged by.

"And," Yogi queried.

"And, what?" I asked.

"And, did the lovely Miss Ward put the moves on you?"

"Shit, Yogi. We aren't going to talk about that. Ok? She did call my house once," I said. "But Emily answered and that was the end of that as far as I know."

"I was sorry to hear about your uncle, " I said after a short pause.

"Yep," Yogi said pondering that situation for a moment. "I was shocked. Hell, the whole department was. Unknown to the rest of us Buford had some bad gambling debts and got sucked into the drug deal so fast he was drowning from the start. He had arranged for each deputy to be away from the department the second day Bruce Sidwell was in the cell. That's how the Mexican was able just to wander in and scare the shit out of the kid. I am sure Buford is also trying to cut a deal because I don't think ex-lawmen fare well in prison."

"Sorry," I offered.

Yogi nodded and skipped a smooth flat slick river rock across the eddy. It barely missed a passing raft. One of the paddlers flipped his middle finger at Yogi. "Go fuck yourself," Yogi yelled back spinning another rock in the direction of the raft. Then he changed the subject, "What about you and Emily."

Smiling and looking deep into the river, like looking into Emily's eyes, I said, "We are in a good place, Yogi. That girl is special. She just may be the one, but there is a lot I don't know about her. Did you know she had been FBI?"

"No shit?" Yogi looked over at me. "No shit?" he repeated, a cracker crumbling from his lips.

"I don't know what the story is, but she was at Quantico at some point before returning here. Someday she may open the window for me about that," I said.

"You know what I can't figure?" Yogi asked.

"What?" I said.

"How a classy chick like that hooks up with a lug like you." Yogi joked.

"She may be nearsighted," I offered.

"C'mon, cowboy," Yogi said punching me on the shoulder, "Come on, race you down to Hell Hole."

I was still thinking of Emily as I strapped in and saw a break in the line of rafts. Then I got my focus back and peeled out into the chute skirting to the right of Witches' Hole and we were off. One with the river.

I didn't even see the two men with cameras standing on the footbridge overhead as we passed through Hell Hole, past the Powerhouse and down to the take out.

The End.

AUTHOR'S NOTE

This is a work of fiction and any reference to actual persons is purely coincidental, however, events similar to these actually occurred during my senior year in college. All of the characters are likewise fictitious comprising parts of many of my fellow students. This book could not have been finished without all those interesting people, living and deceased, who inspired and energized me to write this forty years after the events transpired. I made up the story line about the drugs and Mexicans, but hey, somebody was selling Black Beauties.

ABOUT THE AUTHOR

Jim Cameron is a practicing attorney in Nashville who resides with his wife, and collection of dogs and cats outside Leiper's Fork near Franklin, Tennessee. A graduate of the University of the South at Sewanee and Vanderbilt Law School, he has served as a Boy Scoutmaster, a whitewater canoe instructor, and a board member of the Tennessee Board of Water Quality, Oil and Gas, the Tennessee Wildlife Federation, Tennessee Scenic Rivers Association, and the Better Business Bureau of Middle Tennessee, Inc. He has just completed his second novel in this series, entitled *Hymn for the Cherokee* to be published soon. The second novel poses the question: In the middle of the water war between the States of Tennessee and Georgia over rights to the Tennessee River at Nickajack Lake, what if a document were to be discovered that proved neither Tennessee nor Georgia owned the land in question? Follow Jack, Emily, Yogi and Leon as they commit to search for the treasure, and meet Calvin Moore, the lawyer's lawyer.